# The Angry One

Kyle Rader

# *Also by Kyle Rader*

*My BFF Satan*

*Kegger*

*Four Bullets*

Cover Design, Cover Art by Maciej Kamuda

E-Book Edition ISBN: 978-1-967519-07-1

Paperback Edition ISBN: 978-1-967519-05-7

Hardback Edition ISBN: 978-1-967519-06-4

Burial Books LLC
4000 Eagle Point Corporate Drive
Birmingham, AL 35242
www.burialbooks.com

This is for the fighters. Keep your guards up and chins down. There's many rounds left in you.

# Chapter 1

I NEVER SAW A fighter like Duane Jones.

I was in his corner the night he fought Johnny Montessi; "Johnny the Angel" he was called because of his good looks. Kid could've been in the pictures instead of taking punches for a living. He was also illiterate and couldn't act like anything other than a major entitled prick most of the time. Anyway, he was an up-and-comer, had a record of thirteen wins and no defeats, with six or seven by way of knockout. I'm a bit hazy on the details there, but then again, after the things I saw with Duane, one can hardly blame me. You'll see.

I'd been hired to be the cut man that evening by the promoter, one of the larger four in the Northeast Circuit at the time, this well-coiffed drink of water by the name of Murray Applebaum; Mr. Applebaum to everyone, including his mother, or so the story went. Applebaum had a real eye for talent, that's undeniable. He also had a real eye for money and would do or say anything to get what he felt was his; more often than not, that meant screwing his fighters in the end. Tale as old as time in boxing.

It was supposed to be a tune-up fight. Johnny goes up against someone tough, but not *too* tough to hurt him or, heaven forbid, beat him, and then goes on to face one of the bigger fish. Applebaum had already started negotiations with a rival promoter on the details.

The contract was supposed to have been signed that very night once Johnny the Angel took care of business.

How little we knew.

Duane "The Angry One" Jones was what's referred to as a "journeyman" fighter. Now, a journeyman is a fighter who's got skills enough not to get murdered, but not enough to get put over the top. They fight *all* the time, sometimes taking fights on with as little notice as a couple days. I could name half a dozen guys right now that would fight two, three times a month. They bounce around a lot, promoters sign and fire them as regular as the tide.

"This guy," Applebaum told me as we walked, his arm around my shoulders. He always wore these big, smoked-lensed sunglasses and he smelled of cigars, cologne, and Brylcreem (kept enough of that in his snow-white hair to keep it glued to his scalp). "He's built like a brick shithouse. Got these creepy eyes, green as jade but somehow...kinda black too. You'll see when you meet him. He's rough and tough, so I expect he's gonna try to make it a phonebooth fight. Bad news for him once Johnny gives him a taste of that left hook! Good news for you, Bill! You'll *earn* your check tonight!"

Applebaum took off to go deal with something else, leaving me holding my kit in front of Duane's locker room. I knocked. Silence. I must've stood there like a schmuck for two, three minutes before the door opened up. Creepiest guy I've ever laid eyes on met me on the other side.

"Good evening. I am called Pembrose. I am Mr. Jones' trainer. Please, enter."

Pembrose was the tallest man I'd ever seen. His hair scraped against the ceiling as he walked (man refused to stoop even a little) but it didn't muss up his part at all, not a single black hair was out of place. Man had a face that was tombstone gray and looked like he'd never laughed a day in his life.

The locker room stank. Now, I know they don't normally smell like French perfume, but this place *reeked*. Like someone had moved low tide at Revere Beach inside a musty attic and left it there for a few decades. Christ, even talking about it, I can smell it again...

Duane sat in a metal folding chair, arms hanging between his legs, hands wrapped and gloved, staring straight ahead, but I don't think he was seeing anything at all. Applebaum's description of him was no exaggeration; kid was a *monster!* His arms were the size of my thigh, and his shoulders were broad enough I could've laid down on them and still had room for my dog.

"All right, kid," I said, "let's have a look at you."

I like to get background on my fighters before the bout. Some are talkers and will tell you every little nick and ding they ever had. Others say nothing at all. I hate the braggers, myself, them who go on and on about how great they are and the like. A fighter's face can tell you their life story if you know what to look for. Duane's skin was smooth and clean. I doubted he ever needed to shave more than once a month, if that. His nose was a bit squashed in the middle and slightly crooked, which meant he'd broken it a few times over. I made a note of that as something to prepare for and moved to his eyes. Eye cuts can be the death knell for a fighter, especially along the brow or corner of the eye. Fighters who've been cut before tend to build up a lot of scar tissue, but Duane had nothing. I dug deep too, moving his skin around with my fingers looking for something. It felt...wrong, felt like if I pushed in a bit more his face would burst like a balloon.

"Is something troubling you, Mr. Brava?" Pembrose stood right behind me, stooped at the waist to whisper in my ear. His breath came out in thick waves and the smell moved straight up my nose.

I lurched away, trying not to gag. This is when Duane moved for the first time. Not his body, not his head, just his eyes. Christ, those peepers! So green they glowed. Applebaum was wrong about the blackness though. Not even his damn pupils were that color. They were gray. Flecks of it kinda danced around in the green, gray as a battleship. I found myself looking back into those eyes and wanting nothing more than to run home and call my mother.

I was halfway to the door when a knock came, followed by a hoarse voice telling us it was time to go.

# Chapter 2

<br>

It was at the end of Round Five that everything went bad.

I've seen bad before; part of the gig. Guy comes back to the corner, red stuff painted all over his face, chest, and whatever else the Good Lord gave him. It's my job to patch the fighter up and get them ready for more. When it's really bad, blood gets all over the corner and you got to wipe it up with this nasty bleach concoction before the next round starts. Works good on canvas, but not on skin. Shit'll burn you for hours and won't get any of the red stuff off either, more like it tattoos it in you and you're stuck walking around with some poor schmuck's dried juice for a couple weeks. Nasty business.

Up until those last few seconds, the fight was going exactly as expected. Montessi was showcasing his skills, all but *dancing* around Duane, keeping him at the end of a sharp jab and giving him a double cross if he tried rolling under it. Duane hadn't landed much at all up to that point. He lumbered around the ring, stalking Montessi, trying to get inside and give him the business. He'd managed to time that jab and rush in and tie Montessi up in the center of the ring, pushing him back until they hit the ropes. That's when Duane gave him a double hook to the body that got Johnny's attention. His eyes lit up on the first one—total surprise—and with the second, pain washed over him. It was plain as day for all of us sitting ringside.

Duane had *hurt* him.

They gave the ten-second warning—one of Applebaum's crew knocking on a block of wood—and Johnny Montessi rallied enough to give Duane a reminder of the pecking order. It was dirty, no denying it. Montessi leaned on the back of Duane's neck, pushing him down enough to get him in a headlock. This was misdirection. He knew the ref would break it up, but he'd be preoccupied with untangling him and Duane. Sure enough, as the ref was pulling them apart, the elbow came a-flying, making a sound like out of one of the old cartoons where the dumbass cat gets smashed in the face with a frying pan. Duane staggered backward, holding his face in his gloves. The red stuff was all over the canvas.

Montessi rushed back to his corner, smirking at Duane and thumping his chest with the kinda bravado that was nothing but show. Trust me, the confidence didn't reach his eyes. Anyway, that's when I went to work. The cut was beneath the eye, so I only gave it a moment's glance. Back then, they didn't stop fights for any blood; it was extremely rare anyway. Not to say I didn't treat it, mind you. I jabbed a couple cotton balls soaked in my own mixture of anticoagulants (trade secret, so don't ask) and held it there with my thumb, grinding it in so it'd go to work faster as I focused on the immediate problem: the swelling. Duane's eye was fused shut behind a shield of discolored skin that seemed to be ever-growing. I asked him to try and open it, but he couldn't.

This was bad. Duane would be going out effectively blind on one side. He wasn't supposed to win the fight, sure, but he was supposed to have what they call a "puncher's chance" too. Montessi would hone in on that puffy purple mass and attack until Duane couldn't take it no more and went down or he did permanent damage. You know what? He'd be right to do so too. Our sport isn't for the weak-kneed.

"Mr. Brava?" Pembrose's voice surprised me. The tall manager hadn't said but two or three words to his fighter the entire night; said naught to me. He looked at the state of his man, and then gestured to my belt. "If you please?"

My belt was where I'd keep a couple of razor blades. Back then, a quick and dirty way to resolve a swollen eye was to cut your fighter—very carefully—along the eyelid. In my entire career, I only had to do it a handful of times. If you can't control it with ice and a change in strategy, then you might as well toss the white towel in, was my school of thought. But Pembrose gave me the nod, so I did as I was told.

It's tricky. Go too deep, you risk creating an even more inciting target for your opponent, plus you got another damn cut to manage. Hell, you could even slice through *into* your own guy's eye if you didn't know what you were doing. Fortunately, or unfortunately, I knew what I was doing. I used to practice on things like grapes and bananas to get my control down.

The Angry One weren't no banana.

That smell I told you about in the locker room? The second I stuck that blade in Duane and started dragging it through that purple flesh, it hit me. It was worse than before, more pungent. Back in the war, I saw this officer get blown out of his jeep after it ran over a landmine. Spun in the air before landing on some pointy rocks, those volcanic-type that are all craggy? He lay there while we took fire, screaming and bleeding for hours until he died. We didn't get to his corpse until the next day, after the insects had gotten to it. I thought that was the worse stench a man could ever experience.

Until I smelled Duane Jones' blood.

I tell you here and now, it wasn't...*right*. It was too red. *Way* too red. It looked like paint, not blood, and had roughly the same consistency, but like if it wasn't mixed right, soupy and thick, almost like mud.

I had a hell of a time trying to clear it away so I could see what the hell I was doing, and when I did, stuff smeared all around his face instead of absorbing into my towel. I had to toss a half a bucket of water in his face to clean it all up. As I was putting my solution to the cut—trying to get the blood to clot up quick enough before Montessi started putting leather in it again—Duane's skin...it didn't *move* right. It was loose, like leftover chicken that'd been in the fridge for too long. I had a thought that if I took hold of the corner of the cut and pulled, I'd be able to peel his entire face right off. What lay underneath that mug of his, whatever it was that made him reek worse than the dead, I wasn't sure that I wanted to see.

We don't always get what we want in life, though, do we?

I got the cut right at least. Duane could see out of the eye well enough to keep going and not get murdered out there.

Sorry. Poor choice of words. Given what happened.

I'm getting to that part, the part that was in all the papers back then; still gets talked about today whenever some in-ring tragedy occurs and they bring up the "barbarity" of the sport. Here's something that wasn't in any paper, that no analyst or journalist knows. Pembrose leaned in and whispered something in Duane's ear. I was shlepping my gear out the ring and didn't catch it all. The bit I did hear didn't sound like any language I'd ever heard. I thought it might have been a mix of Russian and Korean. Whatever was said, it *changed* Jones in a way I'd never seen a fighter change in the corner before. Those eyes of his, they lit up, grew so damn wide they nearly popped out of his skull. It was anger. Lots and lots of anger. I never knew a person could keep that much inside them. He rose to his feet and slammed his gloves together so hard that *I* felt the impact in my molars.

I looked at Pembrose before the bell sounded for the sixth. He watched Montessi mugging to the crowd by kissing his fists and biceps;

they ate that stuff up from him. Pembrose had but the one expression—empty—but as he stood there, arms crossed over his chest, I saw the ghost of a smirk haunt his face for the briefest of seconds.

It took twenty-five seconds for The Angry One to finish off Montessi. Five to hurt him, the other twenty to make him suffer.

Think about that. Twenty-five seconds. That's nothing, right? Less than a commercial for goddamn Burger King. And yet, it's also a friggin' whole lot of time too. Standing there, watching it, I experienced it at full-speed and kind of slow-motion at the same time. It was strange, almost like I was outside my body watching it happen.

Christ, imagine how poor Johnny Montessi felt.

Anyway, the bell sounds and Duane barrels across the ring to meet Montessi. Montessi greets him with two stiff jabs that'd bust your nose if he was really putting the juice in, which he was. Duane took the first, then bobbed under the second, coming up on the inside and landing a left hook to the body, *the* hook, for those who were there and remember it, and how it gets written about ever since. It was the best punch of the fight for Jones by far; short, sharp, and clean. The damage was instantaneous. Montessi's face twisted up and he crumpled a bit, curling at the waist and dropping his left to protect himself. Fighter like him, this is where he'd try to dance away, or at the worst, tie up Jones and try to catch a breather. That punch was so vicious, and he was in so much pain, he wasn't thinking strategy. You get hurt in the ring, you think survival like that. The level of hurt that Duane inflicted next? Well, I don't know if you *can* think about anything at all, save for the pain.

Duane sprang up from the body shot and landed a second left hook to Johnny's face. His cheek exploded. I'm not joshing here; it burst apart, blood and shit flying all over the place. The cut was one not even the best of us could have salvaged, the kind where the bone peeks out from under all that meat to say hello. Ref would have stopped the fight were he competent. This one was a two-time loser, a hopeless drunk and gambler long in the pocket of Murray Applebaum. What he saw shocked him not only into inaction, but made him as sober as a priest. Not that you *could* stop Duane at that point. He was already moving on to the next punch. A double right cross crushed Montessi's nose flat against his face and squirted even more blood all over the ring. Johnny stumbled back against the ropes, but was still on his feet, hands up and trying to defend himself, the poor, dumb kid. From there, Duane went to the ol' one-two, landing six straight, each one snapping Montessi's head back like a whip. The reporters and fat cats in the front row didn't realize they were in the "splash zone" and got coated in blood. Have to admit, seeing some of the dames shrieking as red juice got on their Saturday Best and their pearls gave me a bit of a chuckle. Rich people bleed and shit and piss just like the rest of us down in the slums. When the fragility of life gets put in front of their faces, they either freak out like the dames and John Q. Wall Street did or...

...or they act like something else...

Yeah. I'll get there in a bit.

The ref didn't jump in to stop it; he should've though, should've the second Montessi's head started to swell. Big ol' hematoma formed above his left eye socket and kept growing bigger and bigger, giving Duane one hell of a target. The more punches that landed, the harder Montessi's head snapped back. Wet thuds, like loading a side of beef onto the butcher's table. Still, he wouldn't drop. Kid was either too tough or too proud to know he was licked. Duane used that right cross like a cobra, snapping, striking, and snapping back to strike again. The skin of the hematoma turned the color of a ripe blueberry. I found myself clutching the ring apron until my fingers cramped, waiting for it to burst. The crowd too. These people were straight out the Coliseum, demanding more Christians get tossed to the lions and gorillas.

The Angry One hit Montessi with a left hook, followed by another right. Clean as clean gets. Fighters dream about getting to land shots like those. Montessi's eye *leapt* out of his face; dangled in front of his chin like some kind of messed up Christmas ornament.

He screamed then. I still hear it sometimes, at night. I imagine it'll be waiting for me on the other side when it's my time, the doorbell to my own personal Hell.

Montessi dropped to his knees, eye hanging from this pink stalk, blood pouring onto the canvas like lava out of a volcano. He rolled around the ring, screaming, "*Mama! Mama!*" The ref started puking center ring but kept the count going despite tasting his pot roast a second time. By the time he hit ten, Montessi was covered in red. Twenty men jumped in the ring as the bell sounded, doctors trying to help him, photographers trying to get *the* picture that'd see them fed for two months, and lastly Murray Applebaum, and boy, did he look *mad*. He took a single look at his fighter and turned away. Not so much in disgust over the injury, but probably because he knew he was out a small fortune. That's about as much humanity most promoters have, let me tell you.

As for The Angry One? He sat on his stool in his corner, arms hanging between his legs, slumped over and breathing heavy, staring across the ring at the gaggle of people around Montessi. He didn't speak a word, but those eyes of his spoke thousands of pages, each word the same.

*Hate.*

Pembrose patted me on the shoulder, offering me his hand. "Fine work tonight, Mr. Brava," he said. His hand felt like wax paper. He turned to his fighter and began wiping him down with a towel, massaging the knots out of his shoulders. I gathered up my stuff and cleared the ring, heading back to the locker rooms as Pembrose finished up.

As for Johnny Montessi? He didn't make it out of the building; died as they loaded him in the ambulance. All those heavy shots to the head opened a bleed inside his brain that caused him to have a series of strokes. Even if they'd gotten him under the knife, he would've died. Kid never stood a chance. Saw lots of young guys go like that in the war. The older I get, the less sense it makes to me.

Thoughts like that were to be the least of my problems, as I soon found out.

# Chapter 3

Applebaum was livid.

He had a couple of his knuckle-draggers meet me the second I left the ring to escort me someplace more private. Goons weren't too gentle about it either. One of them took my kit and chucked it in a trash can, while the other twisted my wrist behind my back, applying enough pressure as not to break it in two, but to make sure I knew they weren't screwing around.

Believe me, I knew.

They took me to a loading dock and tossed me in a chair in the corner. The bigger of the two held his fist under my nose before he left, making sure I knew to keep my ass glued to that chair. A few minutes passed, and they came back with Pembrose and The Angry One. The hate had gone from Duane's eyes. In fact, he seemed the calmest one out of all of us. He looked at his boxing boots, this bemused expression on his face as he kicked a piece of trash from one toe to the other. I remember thinking: *Who is this guy and where'd they stash the brute who did Johnny Montessi in?*

"What the hell were you thinking?!" Applebaum said to Pembrose. He paced in front of us, dabbing sweat from his forehead as he walked. His goons, loyal to their most recent paycheck, stood behind him; big guys all, arms either crossed or holding onto something inside their jackets. Pembrose said nothing, looked down at Murray as he continued his vulgarity-riddled tirade, eyebrows raised like he was watching an ant scream at him. "You said your boy was tough! That he'd give a good showing but wouldn't be in the same league as my guy! Now, I gotta prospect heading to the morgue! What would you call that, huh?"

"Mr. Applebaum, the specifics of our contract were indeed delivered upon. Young Johnny Montessi, may *God* rest his soul," Pembrose got a little twinkle in his eye when he said that bit—smiling through the eyes is what my ma used to call it, "received quite the challenge, and my man here gave a far-better accounting than anyone, including our dearly departed Johnny, expected. Why, when you look at it from that angle, we exceeded."

Boy, if that wasn't the *wrong* thing to say to the *wrong* person at the *wrong* time, let me tell you! Applebaum, all tanned up, turned a kind of rust color as his blood got up and flushed his face. Add that to his snow-white hair, and he looked like some kind of demon.

"*Exceeded?!*" He reached into his jacket and pulled some heat, the action causing his goons to follow suit. "Exceeded, you smart-mouthed motherfucker?! I'll show you goddamned exceeded! Before I do, though, you're gonna give me the name of the spineless worm who took your action. You too, Bill!" Applebaum pointed his gun at me. Looking down one of them, seeing both the eyes of the man who intends to end your existence and that black eye at the end of the barrel, the indifferent one, the *hungry* one, that doesn't care who it eats, well, my balls shrank right up into me, no lie. I couldn't even tell him I had nothing to do with anything! "Give me the name and I'll make it quick and promise that they'll give you an open casket. Best I can do."

"Perhaps *I* can do better," Pembrose said. That big son of a gun? *His* nuts weren't up in his guts, I'll tell you that. He stepped *into* the gun, hands clasped before his waist like a waiter waiting for the check. "A proposition, Mr. Applebaum, one that will not only reimburse you for the evening's...*tragic* outcome, but far beyond. I daresay it will provide you with more wealth and influence than you've ever imagined."

"Wealth and influence, huh? I already got that, pal! I'm giving you to the count of five to give me a name, then bullets start flying. One."

"You cater to more than the unwashed masses out there, yes? Have a more *elite* set of clientele you provide entertainment for?"

"Two."

"Allow me to put on a match at one of your, shall we say, *events?* My man against one of your most vicious, dirtiest fighters. I shall guarantee a bout not seen since the days of John L. Sullivan."

"Three."

"My fighter shall last as long as *you* deem necessary. Be that two rounds or two hundred, my man shall not fall until it suits you, Mr. Applebaum."

Murray lowered his gun a bit at that. He cocked an eyebrow. "If you and your boy had done what *suited* me, you'd not be about to take a dirt nap, freak."

Pembrose smiled. He had these awful teeth I'd not really noticed before. They were...*twisted* inward, all aiming for the center of his mouth. Brown and green and gray, they looked like moss-covered rocks out in the woods. Applebaum got a snootful of his breath and did *not* care for it; waved his hand in front of his face and coughed, it was so bad. "You run your own book at these private events, correct? You control the *action*, you set the odds, and *you* collect the rewards. For all intents and purposes, you are Plutus there. As such, the proposition I am offering you is to set my man against your bruiser. He shall absorb as much punishment as you require, last as long as you need, and then, when it is most assuredly in your favor, then and only then will he fall. A smart man, a *clever* man should be able to recoup his losses from this evening's tragic events with little difficulty. Perhaps such a smart and clever man would be able to even come out ahead."

I'll be a son of a gun if Applebaum didn't thumb the hammer back and put his gun away; his goons followed suit. "You can't guarantee he'll last," he said. "Guys I line up for those fights eat iron and crap steel. You'd be serving him up, and for what, to save your own keister?"

"What do you think of that, Lumpy?" Applebaum said to Duane. "You like that your trainer is offering you up as sacrifice?"

"Mr. Jones is not a *verbose* individual, Mr. Applebaum." Pembrose walked in front of Duane, blocking him from Murray's view. "He knows what is good for me is also good for him. He will deliver what is expected of him."

"You're kinda nuts, you know that?"

"Do we have a deal?" Pembrose held out his hand. Applebaum took it a second later and gave it one firm pump. He looked at his hand in disgust afterward. He called a goon over and wiped it—front and back—on the man's suitcoat.

"You're sticking with them, Bill," he said to me. "I don't know if you were in on this or if it's a case of rotten luck, but I can't very well let you walk away. You go where they go, sleep where they sleep, shit where they shit. You see *anything* not on the up-and-up, you tell me. You don't?"

Applebaum didn't need to finish the threat. I'd been around long enough to know what happened to people who crossed Murray Applebaum. He and his goons left me there with my new crew. Pembrose nodded to Duane, who rose to his feet and followed the tall man as he walked to the exit.

"Coming, Mr. Brava? Much to do."

# Chapter 4

THAT'S HOW I CAME to live with Duane "The Angry One" Jones and Pembrose.

Turned out, Pembrose was doing all right for himself. He lived in this huge mansion on the outskirts of town. I'm talking fourteen bedrooms, full kitchen like you'd see in a restaurant, servants' quarters, three-car garage, hell, he even had a small orchard on the property, apple and cherry trees mainly.

There was a bit of a caveat, though. The whole place looked like it hadn't been lived in for a generation. Dust lay inches thick on every surface and hung in the air like thick, hot air down Florida way. I couldn't go more than a few minutes without sneezing or coughing. Majority of the furniture was covered with cloth. Most of the lamps had no bulbs; Pembrose handed me a big flashlight the first day, along with a basket of batteries. "This part of the county, I'm afraid the grid is more than a bit...*dodgy*, Mr. Brava. Thus, we try to conserve it for only the *essentials.*"

That orchard I told you about? I went on walks there twice a day—clearing my lungs from all the dander. Most of the trees were dead and rotting, and the ones that still lived had all sorts of problems. Apples in weird shapes, some thin and nail-like, others were coated in what I took to be mold. The cherries were no better. They littered the ground, obese and over-ripe. They'd burst open upon even the slightest disturbance, giving off this awful stink as their juice—pitch black—soaked into the ground. It was the same smell I caught off Duane, off his blood.

Pembrose didn't cheap out on me and gave me one of the master suites. While I had to pull the sheets off the beds and bureaus, the room was—thankfully—mostly free of dust. I had access to my own bathroom and a fireplace to top it all off. Fresh linen, wood, and hot water (oh yeah, the boiler was "under repairs," so it was either freezing cold showers or scalding hot sponge baths) were provided to me every day from one of the numerous servants skulking about the joint. Those people could've been Duane's family. Odd green eyes, same flecks of gray, empty expressions... Christ, they even smelled the same! I tried to talk with them, to be friendly and what not. I've never been in a joint where I was waited on hand and foot before, so I wanted them to know I wasn't all up tight. Any time I tried to strike up a conversation, they stopped whatever it was they were doing, dropped their hands to their sides, and scurried away. Sometimes they'd come back in a few minutes, other times I'd not see a single servant the rest of the day.

"They are a private people, Mr. Brava," Pembrose told me over dinner one night, just me, him, a roast big enough to feed a company of soldiers, and these ancient candles with God-knew-how-many years of wax built up on their handles. They were orange, but when lit, they looked like burning skin. "You are astute in your observation though. They and Mr. Jones share a lineage, although not one I'd call *direct*. Think of them all as distant cousins."

Pembrose went on to explain that they came from the North Shore of Massachusetts, near Marblehead, and that the Jones family had been there since the discovery of the New World and the first real settlements from Europe. "Of course, they quickly discovered that their 'New World' wasn't all *that* new," he said, smirking as roast beef juice ran out the corner of his mouth. "Certainly not to those who had called it home for thousands of years. Not to those who'd been here even *longer* than that. It's a great big world out there, Mr. Brava. Most people don't even realize how so. The things *people* do not know or that have been lost to the great equalizer, Time, are both immeasurable and unimaginable.

"I, myself, come from Salem, my family being amongst the first of the city fathers. It's quite wonderful, that small corner of the globe. The air and water possess a rejuvenating factor akin to the fabled Fountain of Youth! I know in my heart of hearts that I am destined to return there for my final place of rest, but until then? The show must go on, as the saying goes, yes?"

"Begging your pardon, Mr. Pembrose," I said with a mouthful of yams, "but how'd you get into the fight game? A well-educated, worldly sort of person such as yourself, it strikes me as being somewhat beneath your station. No offense meant, of course."

"And none taken, Mr. Brava, none taken, indeed. It is a fair question. It was upon one of my many returns home that the opportunity to enter the *great game* landed in my lap. I had a stopover in a small town along the coast between Marblehead and Swampscott by the name of Rumney; scarcely a town, Mr. Brava. I daresay there wasn't more than two hundred souls living there at its peak. Gone now, of course. The residents absorbed into the surrounding towns, abandoning their native homes for opportunity, the *great* untold American tale. The residents were the poorest of dredges, you understand. Made their living off meager hauls from their lobster traps and fish hauled from the sea, which was not enough to compete with the larger township's business. An ignorant people as well, Mr. Brava, although it was mainly by design and desire. I can see you shifting in your seat as

I say such *incendiary* talk. I am no bigot, Mr. Brava, of that I can assure you. Rumnians are—how can I put it—merely different in their view of life and the world than you or I. They've no schools or use for books or writing, choosing to pass down their knowledge through the grand oral tradition. Fathers teach the sons, mothers teach the daughters, and so on. Being of so few in number, one has to ponder the question of inbreeding, yes, but I shan't bore you with any such tales. You wish to hear of my boxing debut, after all!

"My stopover in Rumney was not a coincidence or one of convenience. I'd heard tales up the Shore, tales of a tough man, one willing to take on all comers in the older tradition of pugilism. No gloves, no round limits. One man against the other in a ring until only one of them walked out. The stories grew more apocryphal in each re-telling, as such things are wont to do, until this man grew to the stature of a Greek demigod, sent down from Olympus to perform some great, unknown deed. I was intrigued, but cautious. One doesn't spend their time living on the Shore without learning to spot a racket, especially when the town of Rumney is mentioned. I told you before they are different, and that is true. They are, as such, for good or ill, treated differently than the normal man. Shunned would be a mild way of phrasing it, the polite way, I gather. The truth is, Rumnians are despised throughout the Shore! They are thought of as 'less than,' parasites, *weird,* who only want to corrupt others to their strange, yet seemingly harmless way of life. Sad state of affairs, Mr. Brava, but I digress.

"I decided to venture to Rumney and find out the truth, to see with my own eyes if he be of living flesh. At first, no one would speak to me, let alone look me in the eye! They scuttled and scurried off to the hovels they crafted out of driftwood and scrap metal, shutting the doors tight behind them. I walked the main drag for a time—there really was only the one road suitable for motor vehicles in town—seeking information, someone to break the taboo of small-town thinking and speak to me, an *outsider*. I saw nothing but contempt and crabgrass, Mr. Brava.

"I was about to give up when I happened upon the general store and saw a bit of a crowd, and not just of Rumnians. There were cars in the lot with plates as far away as Maine and New York. The store had been converted from an old barn and served as the post office, trading post, auction house, and even their church, as so much as Rumnians go in for any *newer* gods. I made my way through the crowd to the forefront. Here! Here, Mr. Brava, was I greeted with the perfume of our trade! Sweat, blood, stale breath, and that wonderful spark of life when our species engages in the sweet science! It made my hair stand on end, made the air taste like fresh peaches. My feet moved me as close as I could go to the action until the coarseness of the makeshift ring-rope rubbed an abrasion into my wrist, halting my progress. It was there that I got my first glimpse of the specimen that I now manage. 'The Angry One,' Duane Jones."

The servants came in at that point and cleared the table. A few minutes passed and they brought in dessert, some kind of orange-crumb pastry which I declined, but Pembrose ate a whole cake of. The man's mouth stretched wider than what seemed possible as he finished it off in two bites. I took some brandy in my coffee after seeing that, let me tell you.

"Duane," Pembrose packed a pipe and absent-mindedly puffed at it after the servants left again; it didn't smell like any tobacco I'd ever smelled before, "was participating in some small, unsanctioned bouts in Rumney and had been for some time. No governing bodies, no judges, no *Murray Applebaums*." He winked when he said our new employer and possible killer's name. "Two men, one referee, and whatever ring they could put together. Very little in the way of *rules*, although they did manage to stick with Queensbury, save for the gloves. This bout was strictly in the theater of Sullivan, save for both fighters had some wrapping around their wrists. The town advertised along the dirt roads and through deliverymen to spread the word, attracting the kind of degenerates one might expect would attend such an event: rock-bottom gamblers, desperate for someone to take their action, low-level gangsters seeking a new racket to exploit and control, and the curious few such as myself, seemingly perfectly *normal*, God-fearing Christians drawn to this dilapidated barn to watch two men beat each other until near-death.

"The bare knuckles bouts of yesteryear possessed a certain elegance, but they often devolved into what I came upon: a slovenly disgrace. Duane's opponent was a bear of a man named Kurtz. A third-generation carnie, he made his way primarily as the strongman, bending metal and lifting impossible weights. He took fights on the side during the carnival's off-season to make extra pocket money. He leaned in the corner as his trainer gave him instructions, wiping the blood, sweat, hay, and sawdust from his bare chest as best he could. Round Fifty-Nine had concluded, with the big Six-Oh coming up. I found it amusing, Mr. Brava. After punching a man for that length of time and he still will not fall, what instruction is there *left* to give?

"Kurtz's face was swollen. He bled from both ears and nose. His mouth hung open as the bell sounded and he lumbered forth to meet Duane. Duane was worse off than Kurtz, worse off than any mortal man I've ever seen, if I may be honest. The top of his skull was swollen black; both eyes had fused shut into dark orbs of twisted, damaged flesh. There was no possible way he could have seen through them, not even after he'd been *opened* up by a dull blade in his corner by the toady he'd engaged as corner-man. His chest was mottled with fist-prints, and a rather large bruise had stretched out from his navel to his hip. Bare knucklers, as you, a student of our game, know, can break their hands aiming for the head, thus grappling and body blows are more expected than naught. This is exactly what Kurtz did at the start of Round Sixty. Two quick jabs and then he stepped in to embrace Duane in the center of the ring. They held each other there for the majority, the one tossing a few hooks and the other returning in kind. Exciting, it was not, and it continued like this for ten more rounds—*ten*, Mr. Brava—before I was properly introduced to 'The Angry One.'

"Something changed in Duane before Round Seventy. You've seen those eyes of his, yes? Green and grey? It was then that I caught my first glimpse of those; underneath all that swollen skin, they appeared, at first, as distant as the light of the very stars above our heads, yet far, far brighter. I felt something in my bowels that made me quite uncomfortable. I daresay I would have regurgitated if I'd held his gaze for longer than that brief instant. I'd forget the sensation, and nearly everything else I'd planned in my life in the next fifteen seconds. I know now what the feeling was, Mr. Brava. It was nothing less than my destiny greeting me.

"Duane shoved Kurtz away as he tried to grapple, ducking under a counter left hook to deliver a short uppercut that snapped Kurtz's head back. He hit him with this again, then a left hook. Kurtz stayed on his feet; I do not know how. Duane elbowed the referee away and descended upon him. The smacks of flesh on flesh, of bones snapping, of air being driven from lungs, it silenced the roar of the crowd until all that was left was the violence. The referee called for the bell, and it took half a dozen men to pull Duane off Kurtz. The fight was over."

Pembrose rose and tapped his pipe against the side of the fireplace. The flames seemed to spark with blue light as the ashes fell to the floor.

"I knew I had to take this specimen out from the backwaters and ghost towns, that there was something special about Duane Jones that the world needed...no, *deserved* to see. I promised him fame and fortune, although his concern was more for the latter; all his winnings went into the Rumney coffers, as they still do. Two short years later, here we are, and here you are, Mr. Brava, the newest addition to our little flock."

"How many men you see him go up against?" I asked. "How many men you see Duane work over like this Kurtz fellow? Like Johnny Montessi?"

"Mr. Kurtz is alive and well," Pembrose said. "He sticks with the carnival; no more bare-knuckle bouts for him. I was told he spent a day and a night in bed and was up and about like nothing happened after that, drinking and carousing and telling the tale of the 'Beast Who Crawled up from the Sea' that he fought in Rumney. Quite the storyteller, that Kurtz. The majority of my promotion work was done well before Duane's first professional bout."

"And Montessi?"

"Sacrifices are sometimes necessary in life, Mr. Brava. In our modern times, we've lost sight of that, lost sight that *we* may be the sacrifice for someone else, for some*thing* else. Johnny Montessi found out that truth before his end. And now, I shall leave you. Best get some rest, Mr. Brava. Lots of work to do tomorrow, indeed!"

# Chapter 5

Not quite the story you thought it was going to be, is it?

You were expecting some old yarn about the ringside view of a couple bouts for some no-name journeyman fighter, and here I am telling you about bare-knuckle brawls and awful-smelling, weird-looking folk and a strange mansion.

It gets stranger from here.

Before I get to the underground fights that Duane fought for Murray Applebaum, I have to tell you about the mansion again. See, I said I had free reign of the house and the grounds, and while that was mainly true, there was one door that remained locked to me until the very end: the basement. I happened to see the door on my first afternoon there, and when I tried to open it, found it locked and didn't think much of it. Weren't my house, Pembrose could lock whichever doors he liked. A few of the servants, the Rumnians, saw me try the door and it weren't but two or three hours later that the basement door was fitted with no less than *four* new locks. Four!

I can take a hint; would've, too, if not for the noises.

They came at night, sometimes in the early morning as the servants were getting the house ready for the day, making breakfast and doing the laundry and the like. I heard it all the way on the third floor of that damned mausoleum. Started as this faint scratching, *gnawing* almost. I grew up in a tenement building, so I chalked it up to mice or squirrels that'd made a home in the walls. But it grew louder, more intense as the days turned to nights and then to weeks and months. It weren't no vermin scratching away, of that I knew. Claws and teeth on wood and plaster don't ring, for one; these noises did. A rhythmic ring, one or two beats after the other, sometimes even more like *clangclangclang-clang* all at once.

It sounded like digging.

I can't even begin to describe the smell. Woke up with my mouth tasting of dead things and sewage. Took to brushing my teeth four times a day and drinking the strongest black coffee to get rid of it, and even then, the memory of it haunted me like a damn specter. Needed two showers and three changes of clothes a day to even *attempt* to keep ahead of it.

During a training session in the gymnasium, while Duane was working the speed bag, I mentioned it to Pembrose. He pushed himself off the ring apron and rose to his full height, looking down the end of his nose at me with those eyes of his. "Renovations, Mr. Brava," he said after a few moments of this, before returning his attention back to Duane. "Nothing more than that. I'll have the servants prepare some nice chamomile tea to assist your sleep at night."

I hate chamomile. And I hate liars more. The little intimidation Pembrose tried to pull on me was his way of letting me know I ought to drop it, should I know what was good for me. Thing of it was? He couldn't touch me, not without upsetting Applebaum even further, and I didn't think he wanted to test out those waters, not before he showed what Duane could do in the underground, so I *didn't* let it go; more like, I filed it away for a later date is all.

God help me, I wish I hadn't.

# Chapter 6

I ended up in Duane "The Angry One" Jones' corner for fourteen underground fights for Murray Applebaum. Each one went exactly as Applebaum wished, down to the number of punches thrown. As seedy and intriguing as the whole set-up was, I only really need to tell you about the first and the last fight. They're the ones I can recall like yesterday, still see when I close my eyes and in my dreams all these decades later. The other twelve I sort of...*endured*, like I was watching myself from a few inches over my body.

The venues changed, sometimes the day of, sometimes a couple hours before! They don't call it "underground" for nothing. Murray Applebaum, for all his bluster, for all his sway, was wary of prying eyes. Sure, he had cops on the payroll, newspapermen too, creating a network of informants that ought to have kept him comfortable enough. The underground fights meant *real* money. I'm talking CEOs, bored millionaires, oil barons, heck, we even had a couple of the Shah's entourage attend with fair regularity (showing my age there, I know; look it up on the internet). Getting busted at one of these would be an embarrassment for those people, maybe a whole political scandal, but nothing they'd suffer serious consequences over. That'd go to Murray. Running unsanctioned, illegal bouts? There goes his license along with a lengthy prison stint and a lifetime ban from the sport. So, his paranoia wasn't entirely unjustified, even if it did make him more of a prick to work for.

This first bout was in the basement of one of his patrons' buildings. They put up signs saying the lower parking level was reserved or under construction or something like that, all the while they had Murray's goons in ill-fitting tuxedos directing limos and Cadillacs right on through. You could *smell* the money that first night. The elite had come out to play, to indulge in something their ancestors might've done in the Coliseum, save for they used to let the *hoi polloi* in to see some poor assholes get eaten by a tiger back then. This was strictly invite-only. You had women in pearls and diamonds worth more than a Joe like me could ever hope to earn in a lifetime, men smoking cigars that were smuggled out of some repressive regime somewhere and cost more than a few lives to get to their greedy, fat lips. And slinking through their personal space was our host, Murray Applebaum, teeth shining as bright as those diamonds. He'd put on a fresh tan and the low light made his face appear hidden in the gloom, but that Brylcreemed hair of his and those teeth? Christ, he glowed like the rising sun in that basement.

"Had a lot of time to ponder the Montessi affair," Applebaum said, holding me by the arm. "I'm still not one hundred percent on you. Hope I'm not misjudging your character."

Duane was paired up with this brick shithouse of a man named Tony White. I don't know where Applebaum found those fighters, but wherever it was couldn't have been nice. Tony towered over Duane, had at least forty pounds on him and it was all muscle. Christ, he looked like someone's masterpiece sculpture, save for this horrible scar over his brow that hadn't healed right. The skin was all...twisted over itself and a different shade than the rest. It looked like someone had tossed their pastrami on rye at him and it took root. I found out later that he got that in a prison riot when, after a guard put another black inmate into a coma, Tony stalked him through the prison until he found him. Bent the racist son of a bitch over his knee until his spine snapped, but the guard managed to slice Tony up in the process.

Boxing's got lots of dark stories like that.

Murray came up to Pembrose and gave him the rundown: three-minute rounds, no gloves, no eye gouging or nut shots. Duane was to give a good enough show to last through fifty rounds. "Fifty rounds." Applebaum jabbed his finger into Pembrose's chest. "No more and certainly not less. Your boy does that, then maybe we'll see how far on the road to square you and me are."

It was my job to keep him patched up and on his feet to ensure the show went on. One good thing about it being unsanctioned was that I could pull out all the illegal tricks I'd learned in my time: like a *Break Glass in Case of Emergency*-type of deal. Pembrose got me everything I asked for, without question. I mixed this asthma medication into one of the water bottles. Stuff is basically a steroid, and when it hits your system, it's like a jump-start, clears your lungs right up, helps the fighter take in more air, and gives them a feeling of rejuvenation. Problem is, it doesn't last long, and if you overuse it, you run the risk of your man thinking he's goddamn invincible and then he goes out and does something stupid. I also had a couple small vials of cocaine in case Duane ended up dead on his feet. Sniff of this, he'd be wide-awake and ready to go, for a little while at least. You gotta understand, my life was on the line here. I'd never trade in narcotics, but I didn't want to end up on my knees staring up at Murray Applebaum from behind the long black barrel of his gun.

We didn't have gloves, so fixing those was out. Time was you could rub a little something on the ends and instruct your fighter to get in a clinch and work whatever it was into the other guy's eyes, blind or confuse him, depending on what it was. We were allowed to wrap Duane's wrists, that was all, but I kept another bottle handy that could possibly find its way onto his fingertips should the need arise. It was weak enough that it'd wear off in a round or two, but it'd make Tony White feel like he was floating in the ocean and give Duane the chance to recover and keep the rounds piling up.

The fight started with both of them standing in the ring, no ropes, only parked cars and rich people ready to see their lessers fight and struggle for their amusement. They were quiet at first; dead quiet. You could feel it in the thick, dusty air down there. They were *afraid*. Sure, they may have caused a lot of suffering amassing their wealth, buying and selling people without a moment's hesitation or remorse and that stuff, but to see human suffering and look it in the face? Well, all of a sudden, these people got a bit of the ol' Fear of God in them. Oh, it didn't last long. Once the fight was underway and the blood was flowing, they lost any fear for their mortal souls and gave in to the bloodlust, the excitement of the sport.

It happens.

Tony White was no joke. He punished Duane for the first ten rounds, bouncing stiff jabs off his face as he advanced, only to tie him up and lean on him. He'd shove him against a car and sit there for a few seconds as Duane struggled to relieve the pressure with some hooks to the body. Tony shrugged those off with a wide grin he flashed to the crowd, which they ate up. The ref would break them up and Tony would go right back to it: jab, jab, jab, and lean. Rinse and repeat. Duane wasn't able to make it very interesting, and the crowd (and Applebaum) was growing a bit restless. I mean, they paid big bucks to see something unique and savage, and the type of fight we were giving them was more of the old drunk uncle at the tavern variety and we had forty more rounds to go.

In the twelfth, I worked my ass off on Duane's nose. I'm talking I had two fingers jammed up there to the second knuckle moving his cartilage around, it was that broke. They don't really let you do that anymore. Blood ran down past my elbow, drip-drip-dripping onto the floor next to this oil stain. Other than the nose, Duane was mostly okay. The swelling under his eyes was manageable, but it'd grow worse the longer the fight went on, so I figured an appointment with Dr. Blade would be in the near future.

As I straightened out his nose, I gave him some of the cocaine. Believe it or not, it helps with coagulation as well as temporarily numbing the pain. If he felt anything at all, Duane didn't show it. His eyes stared straight forward at Tony White. He'd developed this little spasm under his right eye, and he clicked his tongue against his mouthguard. I didn't notice it in the Montessi fight, but would come to recognize it. "The Angry One," you see, was getting *very* angry.

Pembrose leaned into his ear and whispered some instruction; I couldn't make any of it out once again. Duane sniffed in deep, inhaling blood through his shattered nose (which, let me tell you, is like breathing in razor wire), and went out for the round. He walked right into a right cross that wobbled his knees. A left hook finished the job and down went "The Angry One." Boy, did the crowd roar! It got louder as they realized that Duane was sitting in a puddle of his own blood. The left hook had opened a cut on his eye that I can only describe as a "gusher." The ref? Well, he counted the longest, most lackadaisical count you'd ever heard, eyeballing Applebaum every time he rose his hand for the next number. I was looking over at him too, and also the nearest exit. I didn't know if Duane was going to get up. He sat there, breathing heavy and spitting into the puddle of blood until the ref counted to seven, and then he got up, bouncing around as if it were Round One.

"Remember, Mr. Jones," Pembrose called out from the corner. It was a whisper, if that. Nobody but me and Pembrose could've heard him, *should've* heard him, but by Christ if Duane didn't turn his head and give a nod.

Tony White, maybe sensing he was in for an easier night's work than he expected, gave Duane the bum rush, had him all but bent over backward over the hood of this beautiful Rolls, hammering him with hooks. He didn't care where he landed or how clean, only that he did. The richies were *into* it. Each hook garnered an appropriate '*Ooh!*' Chants of "*Get him!*" changed over to "*Kill him!*" with an ease that anyone of us who claims to be human should be ill-at-ease by. Duane leaned forward, trying to tie Tony up, but Tony shoved him back and hit him with another left hook to the head. Bam! Duane's down for the second time. This time, Tony starts mugging to the crowd, raising his arms, beating his chest, screaming about how he's the baddest man alive. They ate it up; their cheers became an unintelligible roar. The count's going—little bit faster this time. Applebaum started reaching into his jacket for the butt of his pistol; his goons were closing the space between me and the exit. And Pembrose? He's standing there, fingers tented under his nose, watching his fighter bleed more than a butchered hog.

Duane got up at the count of eight and the round ended a few seconds afterward. He was even worse than I thought. I'd have to reset his cartilage again, but the cut over his eye was ugly. His skin opened and closed like a hungry mouth, swallowing the gauze whole, only to belch it back out a second later, soaked red and useless. "Gotta give him the stuff or he'll bleed himself out." Pembrose nodded and I got my special mix ready (still a trade secret. Nice try!) when something caught my attention in the wound, and it wasn't how bad Duane stunk (he did; worse than the Montessi fight). Instead of the pink and red of muscle and sinew I expected to see, it was like...it was like there was *another* layer underneath Duane's skin. It was hard to see in the lights of the parking garage, but when Duane moved his head, something *glimmered* deep underneath, like sunken treasure catching the gleam of some diver's flashlight.

Duane didn't even wince when I gave him my mixture. It'd stop the cut for a spell, but only if Tony White would give it the time to help Duane's blood to clot. After I gave him another snoot of cocaine, I rubbed some of my other mystery bottle onto his thumbs and the backs of his hands. It stank almost as bad as he did and, fixed fight or no, I figured there'd be one hell of an uproar should one corner be caught doing something *nefarious*. "Tie that big bastard up and work this into his eyes," I told Duane before he set out. "Make sure you hold it there for a second or two before you let up."

Duane turned away from staring off into the nothing only he could see and blinked. "Okay, Bill."

*Okay, Bill.*

First words I'd ever heard "The Angry One" speak. I nearly fell on my ass right there—would've, too, if not for Pembrose catching me by the shirt collar. The pictures that exist of Duane Jones don't do that voice any justice. I mean, go ahead and look them up and tell me he doesn't look like some kind of simpleton. A monster. His voice? Soft, elegant, even. And *old* somehow, much older than he claimed to be (he'd have been around twenty-one or twenty-two at this time).

My mystery potion did its job, as did Duane. Tony slowed down to a crawl shortly after Duane tied him up in the thirteenth. He staggered around throwing lazy jabs and clinching when Duane came inside. It didn't appeal to the crowd much, but it let that cut clot enough so it wouldn't be much of an issue anymore. Duane looked sharper too, but so would you fighting against someone who'd been given a Mickey like that.

We were in the late rounds when the woman jumped into the ring. I forget her name—Dolores, I think. She was from old money; you know, one of them families that get airports and museums named after them? Drunk off her ass, she shoved the referee aside and demanded everyone's attention. "You boys have put on quite the show," her words stumbled over her tongue as she spoke, along with the ninth martini she'd had that evening. "However, I must *in*-sist on some *real* action in this round! That said: to whichever man knocks the other down *first*, I shall spend the night with!"

To sweeten the deal, or maybe to show how serious she was, Dolores pulled her breasts out of her cocktail dress and flashed both Tony and Duane, much to the delight of the crowd. A couple of Applebaum's goons escorted her out of the ring as she tripped all over herself trying to tuck them away. The couple of fellows that she was with didn't look none too happy about the deal. Tony White rose to his feet, snorting and stomping like one of the Pamplona bulls. I thought about putting some more of my potion on Duane's hands, but I didn't think he'd get the chance to use it. Tony was fixing to run right across the ring and put Duane *through* the concrete.

Duane though? He wasn't looking at Tony, me, or Pembrose at all. He was looking at Dolores as she was placed—somewhat forcibly—into her seat. She cursed Applebaum's goons, her boy toys, and demanded another drink, swaying like a reed in a breeze as they poured her one. I tell you, Duane showed emotion, *real* emotion, as he watched her. Could have been he'd never seen a naked woman before, certainly not one who looked like Dolores; I never got the chance to ask him. I don't believe it was love at first sight, don't believe in such fantasy at all. I *do* believe in lust. I *do* believe in loneliness, desperate,

desperate loneliness. I think that's what was going through Duane's mind, that and the belief that Dolores intended to follow through with her drunken wager, that it was anything but the outburst of a bored elite wishing to capture a bit of the spotlight for herself. It gave him some hope. That hope though? It damn near cost us everything.

Pembrose didn't even get a chance to put in his mouthpiece. Duane was off the bench and into the ring a second after the bell sounded. Tony White laughed and ran to meet him. He dropped his arms, inviting Duane in, hoping to use that enthusiasm as a trap for his right cross. Duane bobbed inside and, as he was coming up, he stopped and bobbed the opposite way, making Tony miss, and miss bad.

It sounded like a *pop*, the right Duane hit him with. The follow up struck a face so soaked in blood it sounded like the Sunday roast being tenderized. Tony's hands fell to his waist. His mouth hung open. He swayed on his legs. His eyes kept rolling up into his skull. The crowd screamed for more and Duane was all too happy to oblige them. Using his left arm to size it up, Duane teed off another right cross, perfect punch. Hit Tony right in the sweet spot between the chin and the cheek and spun him completely around. He landed face-first on the pavement. Christ, what a sound. You could hear the bones breaking in his face. Blood pooled out from underneath him, moving fast, *real* fast. Some of the Richie-riches had to scoot back as to not get their shiny shoes contaminated by it.

Duane walked back to the corner, staring at Dolores. She looked non-plussed about the whole thing, was having one boy toy light her cigarette and the other refill her glass. She winked at Duane, even blew him a kiss.

I was close to pulling my hair out. Applebaum and his goons had worked their way through the crowd to get right next to us. Applebaum's hand was no longer in his jacket. It was by his side, drumming his fingers on the handle of his pistol. If Tony didn't beat the count (and for the first five seconds, he didn't move at all; didn't appear to even be breathing), we were cooked.

Pembrose didn't seem to notice the threat or care much about it at all. He tended to Duane, wiping sweat and blood from his face, giving him sips of water. All the while the goons closed in. The bullets, cold and indifferent, were seconds from ripping through our skulls.

As the referee nervously counted seven, Pembrose wrung out the towel into his hand, collecting a soapy, pink-tinged mess. He flicked the water into the ring, whispering that same strange language I heard him speak to Duane. A few beads hit Tony and, as the count reached eight (the ref, being in on it, was performing his duty in a very...*lethargic* fashion, if you catch me), Tony stirred. It was like someone let loose a nest of angry hornets in his shorts and they'd started stinging his balls. He pushed himself up to his knees, then sprang to his feet, staggering around the ring, wide-eyed and disoriented, but not in the way a fighter who'd been knocked out cold does when he comes around. That generally takes a couple seconds, and you get a weary sluggishness that you got to either work through or throw the towel in over. Not Tony White. He was lightning in a bottle. If not for the state of his face, he'd have looked as fresh as he did in Round One. He'd broken his orbital bone and jaw, both swollen up to disfiguring levels. Normal fight? He'd be done for. But there was nothing normal about this fight.

The round ended with little fanfare and not much further action. My treatments were holding up, for the most part. We were coming up to the Fiftieth Round, thank Christ. Pembrose leaned into Duane and said, "It's time, Mr. Jones. Do what is expected of you."

Duane pointed over at Dolores, now looking rather bored and listless. Pembrose shook his head, smiling softly. "No, Mr. Jones. Now is not the time for that."

Duane's eyes flashed at that. Those flecks of gray burned bright. He clicked his tongue against the guard. I felt my guts cramp as he walked out to meet Tony, thinking, *Christ, it's Montessi all over again.*

Turned out I needn't have worried. Duane made a good show for a minute and then dropped his hands enough to give Tony White the opening he needed for the big finish. And *what* a combo it was! A stiff jab, followed by a left hook that sent blood high enough it covered the overhead light, dyeing the garage this sickly red. "The Angry One" fell on the ground, staring at his own blood dripping down on him as the ref counted him out.

# Chapter 7

Applebaum came to the mansion a couple days later, smiling from ear to ear. I was the one to greet him after one of the nameless servants let him in. After the fight, Pembrose took Duane into the basement and hadn't emerged since. "Convalescence, Mr. Brava," he said after he ordered his servants (it took six of them to carry Duane) to bring him down the stairs. "That is all Mr. Jones requires at this time. Should I have need of a cut man for that, you'll be the first to know." All I had for company during that week were the strange digging sounds and the stink, which had gotten so bad I'd stolen a few spoonfuls of coffee from the kitchen, shoved them in a plastic bag, and fastened it to my face so I could sleep at night.

"Have to admit, I had my doubts, Bill, but your boy pulled it off and did a man's job of it!" Applebaum reached into his jacket and handed me three envelopes, one for me, one for Pembrose, and one (smallest of the bunch, mind you) for Duane Jones. "Never had such a wild affair, Bill, not in all my years in the business. That boy of yours is quite the find. He's got real sand! How's he doing? Need me to send over my doctor? He's a bit of a rummy, but he's got a sure hand still."

I lied and said that Duane was resting up, but fine. Applebaum nodded and walked around the foyer of the mansion, taking in the abandoned nature of it. His nose turned up in disgust as he got some cobwebs on his jacket sleeve. "Listen, Bill. How soon can you get him ready for another fight?"

"Why are you asking me, Mr. Applebaum? I'm a cut man, not a trainer," I said.

Applebaum put his big, tanned arm around me and pulled me close. Christ, I can still smell his aftershave mixing in with the Brylcreem, almost see how the hairs on his arm got bleached white from the tanning booth. "Bill, you don't understand. You're *my* guy now. You think I trust that walking skeleton? Not for a minute! You're my eyes and ears now. You report everything you see back to me on the reg, understand? If your boy is favoring his dominant hand, I wanna know. If he's packing on the pounds, I wanna know. If he has an irregular *stool*, I wanna know! You understand me now, Bill?"

I nodded. It didn't take a genius to know what he was getting at. Applebaum wanted to know everything about everything as to fix the odds in such a way he could make the most on his return, determine if it made more sense to let it be a clean bout or have one of his guys take a dive. It's the not-so-sweet part of the science, but for them who control the rings, it's the most important.

Applebaum gave me a squeeze I'd feel hours after he'd gone and lit a cigarette as he walked toward the front door. "Something else, Bill," he said through a cloud of blue smoke. "Probably nothing, but it's been on my mind all day long. Remember that broad who flashed her cans? Said she'd bang the next man to knock the other down to Kingdom Come?"

"How could I forget?" I said.

Applebaum grunted a humorless laugh and nodded. "Funny thing, seems she's gone missing."

"Missing?"

"Yeah. She and those two muscle heads she had hanging off her that night. Funnier yet? No one seems to have any clue as to where she might have gone, especially without her car. They found *that* on the side of one of the old rural routes, about ten miles in the *opposite* direction of her penthouse, keys still in the ignition."

I started to feel a coldness working its way up my leg like a spider made from ice and burrowing into my guts. "That's very odd, Mr. Applebaum," I said, chuckling and giving a weak shrug. He stared at me through a film of smoke and tinted glass, saying nothing. "Maybe she got a ride from somebody? Took off on some spur-of-the-moment trip to Paris?"

Applebaum sucked the rest of his smoke down and dropped the smoldering filter on the carpet. "Maybe you're right, Bill. It feels wrong though. People of that *caliber* don't disappear like that. Then again, she's young and of the means where an impromptu trip with two young men to some foreign locale isn't *out* of the question. Nah, I'm going on. I'm sure she'll turn up.

"Remember what I told you, Bill. I'm counting on you here," Applebaum said.

I was alone for a while after that. I went for the morning paper, tearing through it to see if there was anything about Dolores being missing. There wasn't. I guess her family wanted to keep it quiet as to avoid any kind of scandal. A scandal had serious repercussions, everything from loss of business to outright social shunning. Still, though, I had this sinking feeling in my gut about the whole thing. The way Duane looked at her after he'd knocked Tony down, the expectation... I worried that it might've driven The Angry One into that place where his eyes flash over gray and his tongue clicks against the roof of his mouth.

Reading further, I found something strange. While there was no mention of Dolores, there *was* a story about a young factory worker who'd vanished after her shift. She was a nobody, a single woman trying to make her way in the world who lived with her brother in a crappy apartment downtown. She'd not been seen or heard from in two weeks and the brother was beside himself; she was all he had. The police claimed to be looking into it, but you could read between the lines easy enough. They'd taken the report and filed it away and would only bring it out again once her body was found in an alley or lying amongst the tall grass outside of town.

That wasn't the strange part. The article mentioned that the brother walked the route his sister took every day to and from work and, in doing so, noticed a foul smell near the Lucas Bridge unlike anything he'd encountered before. "It smelled like the worst kind of death," he said. He looked under the bridge with the police, but found nothing, not even a dead animal.

The servants kept the old papers, piling them in stacks near the main fireplace on the first floor. I tore through a month's worth. About once a week, there were stories of women who'd up and vanished. No clues, no notes, nothing to indicate that they'd met with any kind of foul play, yet they were...*gone.* Altogether, there had been seven that I could find; ten if you counted Dolores and her boy toys. Only one other witness mentioned a foul odor—the husband of one of the earliest missing women claimed it filled their apartment and he'd had to open all the windows for two days to get rid of it.

I knew that smell.

# Chapter 8

I had to get into that basement.

If Duane was taking women, that'd be the only place he'd be keeping them, *if* they were still alive. I didn't know, but I owed it to their loved ones to try, right? Problem was, even *if* Duane was taking them, and even *if* they were down there, what was I going to *do* about it? They didn't call Duane "The Angry One" for nothing. If he wanted, he could have torn any man apart, limb by limb, without breaking much of a sweat. Not to mention Pembrose. Between the two of them, I wouldn't have made it out alive.

This isn't a good look for me, I know, but I kept my mouth shut; didn't call the cops, didn't even mention it to Applebaum. The way I had it figured is that I had nothing; no proof, no bodies, nothing. I ran to the cops, they'd either laugh me out of the station or come and do a cursory look around the place, giving Pembrose the chance to sweet-talk them into leaving before they decided to check out the quadruple-locked basement. I ran to Applebaum? Well, Applebaum would most likely decide that discretion would be the better part of valor, so to speak, and I'd once again find myself staring down the barrel of his gun.

The gift of time passing, the *curse*, is that of hindsight. Knowing what I do now, I might've been better off with option B.

But I digress.

I kept my head down and mouth shut those next few months, assisting in Duane's training. Mostly I'd handle the mitts and run him through footwork drills, keep time on the speed bag. His wounds from the White bout hadn't simply healed, they were *gone*. His skin was smooth and young as if he'd been born the day prior. I made a remark on this while I was giving Duane a rub down after he'd skipped rope, and he rose and left the training room without a word. "Our Mr. Jones is a scant sensitive about his appearance, Mr. Brava," Pembrose said. "In case you hadn't noticed, Rumnians have a rather...*unique* look about them, yes? Rather *toad-like*, no? Especially about the face? Rumors of inbreeding have plagued them for generations. Why, you even whisper the word around a Rumnian, you're liable to meet with a sudden, violent end!"

"That don't explain his healing," I said. "There isn't even any scar tissue!"

"One of the many wonders of the town of Rumney, Mr. Brava, one not known by many outsiders, certainly not believed by the wider world. Lots of possible explanations lie out there. Some unknown property in their water supply, a veritable fountain of youth granting them longevity and healing properties far beyond you or I, the eugenic aspect, of course, how generations of their *selective* breeding, shall we say, has sparked a new wave of human evolution, and then, there's the more fantastical, the deals with various devils or demons, that the entrance to Hell itself lies beneath Rumney and all are nothing more than the results of demon-human interbreeding. Preposterous, of course. A study was done by a more adventurous professor from one of the large universities down Boston way. Poor chap did his best, but was met with resistance and eventual shunning by the entire town. The conclusions he *was able* to reach made no mention of superstition or selective breeding. He was of the opinion that it was a third-party influence (something was *indeed* in the water), but further study was deemed to be unworthy of the time and effort. I have a copy of the study in the library, should you be curious."

The library soon became one of the few places in the house I was allowed to go unattended. I couldn't even wipe my ass without two of the Rumnian servants standing outside the door, waiting for me to get it done. I took my meals there (unless invited to the main hall by Pembrose) and read through the papers and skimmed the many, many dusty tomes on the shelves. The shelves reached the ceiling on every wall, at least twenty feet high. There was a modest writing desk and a big, overstuffed chair that I claimed as my throne. Pembrose had books on almost everything you could think of, put on the shelves in no discernible order. I found an odd sense of comfort in the chaotic nature and grew to enjoy perusing the shelves for something that would catch my interest. I never knew if I'd find a book on dinosaur fossils, a collection of Greek poetry, or the autobiography of some forgotten nobleman from Europe. It was kind of fun in a way, probably the only real joy I had living in that prison of a house.

One day, this old book fell off the shelf as I was trying to grab a copy of *Tom Sawyer*. Now, when I say old, I mean *antediluvian*. The title: *On Lemuria: Thoughts, Theories, and the Truth on the Lost Continent.* I'd never heard of such a place, real or not. I'd heard of Atlantis, of course; plenty of funny books I read as a kid featured the legendary undersea kingdom, but never Lemuria. I took the yellow-paged tome, sat on my throne, and started reading. Dust motes flew off every page. Every time I turned one over, I was worried it was going to crumble in my hands. The paper had this odd amber tint to it and gave off a sweet smell like pipe tobacco.

The book read like an academic paper: dry, meticulous, yet not without a sense of style, almost enthusiastic. The author was credited as a G.K. Norris, but their academic credentials weren't listed. The print was small, putting my tired old eyes to the test. Many people had written about Lemuria, everything from it being the true Garden of Eden to the home of a "missing link" of humanity. No one agreed as to where it used to lie before some great cataclysm sank it into the briny deep. Some said the Indian Ocean, others the Pacific. Norris' speculation leaned toward it being off the coast of Madagascar and stretching near to Thailand. As to the cataclysm, it was *his* "esteemed opinion" (one he didn't back up with more than a bucket-load of hyperbole and rather salty language toward his rivals; called Blavatsky a "tired, cigarettey fraud") that it was caused by the Lemurians themselves.

*"As no doubt the Lemurians were a brilliant race, possessing of far greater intellect than modern man, they were also possessed of the shared trait of hubris. Like Icarus before them, they flew too close to the sun, and the cost was the entire extinction of their race and society. Their Great Experiment, further, brought about the end of the great lizards—the colloquial term being 'dinosaurs'—that they created and bred for servitude."*

As to what the "Great Experiment" was, Norris had this to say:

*"Beings of longevity far outlasting that of an average, healthy human, the Lemurians were not immortal, and were thus vulnerable to the same methods of expiration as we are today, disease, old age, and violence being their greatest of concerns. As a race, they focused their efforts on solving this in the Great Experiment. Although their methods are long lost to us, history shows us that forces beyond our comprehension were not unknown to them, forces we would call 'magic.' The Lemurians could move mountains upon a whim, make water potable anywhere, and create and control lesser beings. It is the latter that they used as fodder for the Great Experiment. Through careful, selective breeding and through their so-called 'magics,' the Lemurians were on the verge of*

*immortality. Would they have succeeded if not for their greatest enemy, themselves? We shall never know."*

I was bored enough to read the whole thing, but I certainly didn't believe a word of it. I was about to put it back on the shelf when the back page gave way, revealing some pages that had come loose from the binding. These were illustrations: a map of where Lemuria might have been, some symbols that might have been their alphabet, and a sketch of what they might have looked like.

The sketch was a dead ringer for Pembrose.

# Chapter 9

THE FIGHTS WE DID for Applebaum, the next thirteen, were about as bloody and vicious as the first one. Sometimes they were fast, sometimes as long as the White fight, although that was the longest Applebaum required of Duane. It turned out his clientele grew weary if the fights went more than twenty rounds. "Violent, quick, and bloodier than Wake Island" is what Applebaum wanted. Some fights Duane even got to win, enough to make the customers realize he wasn't some punchy fighter Applebaum picked up off the floor from some gin joint.

Duane beat his second opponent in six rounds. He broke the poor bastard's jaw in three places and the guy wouldn't get off his stool after that.

His third was a loss and a longer bout; twenty-two rounds before Duane took the dive. By the end, both men looked like the mangled corpses I saw lying in ditches in Korea.

Fourth and fifth fights were losses. They weren't overly memorable, but I recall that the guy he fought in the fifth busted his hand on the top of Duane's head (I'm talking fingers bent in angles they ought not to be) and he had to "beat" Duane with the one good one.

Duane got to win in fight six and did so in huge fashion. Fought a guy by the name of Danny Chabot out of Rhode Island. Duane's eyes were flashing gray and his tongue was a-clicking the instant he stepped into the ring (a for-real one that time; Applebaum rented out some conference room in a hotel and set it up). In the tenth, Duane shoved Danny Chabot to the ground and hit him while he was trying to rise—left hook to the temple. Instant trip to Slumberland.

Applebaum was a bit pissed by that showing, so Duane had to pay penance in fights seven, eight, nine, *and* ten. He was torn up worse and worse after each loss, and Pembrose would retreat with him into that goddamn basement for a few days before I'd see either one again. The stench was at its peak during this period. I had to bust out one of the windows and sleep on the roof to escape it. When I did spy them again, Duane Jones looked younger. No traces of my stitching to be found.

The less said about fights eleven through thirteen, the better. Duane was actively trying *not* to hurt the bums they put him against. Crowd booed like crazy when there wasn't any blood, so Pembrose instructed Duane to fight dirty, scratching, biting, using elbows, anything to get the red flowing, you know?

The last fight I told you I remember as clear as the first, and the reason for that is beforehand, Applebaum came to Pembrose and me and explained that things were going to go a bit differently.

This time out, he wanted Duane to kill his opponent.

"I wanna see this bum get done like Montessi!" Applebaum was animated as he spoke, his hands flailed, his eyes were wide behind his tinted glasses. Even his famed coiffed snow-white hair was out of place. "I wanna see 'The Angry One' unleashed, you understand? No holds barred! Show these silver spoon bastards what *death* truly is!"

Pembrose nodded along, saying nothing. The ghost of a smirk at the corners of his mouth, the same that danced around in the twinkle in his eyes, said it all.

I didn't want any part of it. What happened to Montessi, horrible as it was, was still an accident. This was out and out murder! Still, did I say anything? Or did I stand there in the foyer, crumpling my hat in my hands watching Applebaum leave and let the dissent die on my tongue?

I'm truly a coward and I'll be damned for it. But there are worse things than to be damned. *Far* worse.

The fight took place in a penthouse suite downtown. There was to be no ring, no ref. Two men standing in a living room, a space larger than most houses and that cost more than most people would ever have. There was an excitement in the air amongst the elite that night; you could see it on their faces. They were about to experience something *forbidden* and wrong, and they were eating it up.

Duane's opponent was no bum. Big guy from deep in the Balkans who spoke zero English and knew nothing but violence since he was three years old. Applebaum, acting as P.T. Barnum that night, couldn't pronounce the guy's name, so he called him "Ivan the Terrible"; real original, I know.

I don't even remember the poor bastard's real name...

Anyway.

Ivan was around the same height and build as Duane, except he looked chiseled out of stone. Nary an ounce of fat on him. You could hear his muscles straining as he warmed up. His eyes were almost as scary as Duane's. You know the kind? There's this *sharpness* to how they look at you, *through* you, as if you are nothing and will *become* nothing should you persist in bothering their owner? Ivan had those. Hell, I doubt it took much convincing to take on a fight to the death. He may have even volunteered.

Applebaum spun the tale for the evening. "A fight to the death, ladies and gentlemen! No time limit, no referee, no rules! Two men pitting their strength and will against one another! In this corner, a man you've not seen in my fights before, one brought from deep behind the Iron Curtain. He watched as the godless Reds lined his family against a wall and gunned them down at the tender age of three. From that day forth, violence would be all he knew, and he would become a scholar in all of its intricacies. Now, he turns his attention to the ring, to the noble art of boxing, to test his mettle. I give to you...IVAN THE TERRIBLE!"

Before he did Duane's intro, Applebaum flipped open this gaudy pinky ring and took a sniff of the contents. White powder clung to the clammy skin under his nose, but no one seemed to care, some even cheered when they saw him do it. Guys like him, it's a matter of time before the life catches up to them. Drugs, booze, broads, gambling, their vices will always overtake them. With Applebaum, they probably would have too; he'd have died in jail or from a rival's bullet in due course had he not followed me into that basement.

There I go again. Getting ahead of myself.

Ivan and Duane started the fight very slow. Duane took on a rather unorthodox stance, where he kept his hands down low, hovering near his navel. This is stupid in many ways, biggest one being, you're all but ringing the dinner bell for your opponent to come on in and bounce some stiff shots against your face. Ivan didn't bite. They circled each other, snapping off jabs here and there, feeling each other out. For a minute there, it felt like a legitimate boxing match instead of a deathmatch.

That ended the second Ivan kicked Duane in the stomach.

Duane reeled backward, but Ivan was on him, throwing tight hooks to his skull. Duane didn't have time to get his hands up and took four in succession before falling onto his face. Ivan backed off him, but not before kicking him in the ribs twice. Christ, his legs cut through the air with this loud *snap*. Duane rolled into a ball. With no count, he had as much time as he wanted to get off the ground, but with no rules, Ivan could easily jump on him and bash his head in. But he didn't. He walked to the other side of the room and crouched down, staring at Duane, waiting. Guy was cold.

Duane took his time getting to his feet. He cracked his neck and rolled his shoulders and next thing you knew, he was across the room pummeling the big Slav. I'd never seen him move that fast, ever, not even when he was out doing his road work. Ivan had his guard up, so Duane worked the body, sending hook after hook into his stomach. The crowd winced after each blow, sucking air through their teeth or cheering to encourage the violence along. Ivan took the shots pretty well. He tied Duane up, spun him around, and pushed him away, only for Duane to duck under a jab and start attacking again. Duane landed ten hooks in a row—*ten!* This was pretty unprecedented, but I had to remind myself, these guys weren't fighting for points or saving anything for the later rounds. There was only the one, and to lose it meant to lose everything.

Ivan put Duane in a headlock and caught a bit of a breather. His mouth hung open as he gulped air and looked off in the distance, past the jeers and cheers of the elite, through the walls of the penthouse to something far off, something only he could see. You get this from a lot in fighters who ought to have hung it up; *punchy* is the term. Ivan was far from that, but I think he was starting to realize that Duane wasn't going to roll over. He walked backward, pushing through the crowd to the nearest wall, and proceeded to punch a hole in the sheetrock, using Duane's *head* as the battering ram. Christ, what a sound...like knocking your knuckles against a big oak tree. Duane was covered in plaster when Ivan pulled him out. He let loose of him only to send him to the ground with a right cross. Blood flew as the punch sent Duane's lips into his teeth, shredding them.

The crowd *loved* that, started a cheer of "Hip-Hip-Hoorah" as the lucky few wiped the gore from their cheeks with silk handkerchiefs. Ivan grabbed Duane by the hair and sent punch after punch into his face, each one a knockout blow in and of itself, and yet, Duane remained conscious. Ivan's hand was dripping wet with blood, and when he brought it down on Duane's face, it made this smack like a mop, soaked with water, hitting a tiled floor.

Roars of "Kill him!" and "Crack his skull open!" filled the room. The crowd edged closer, despite the stink of Duane's blood hitting their upturned noses, elbowing and shoving each other for a better vantage point. It made me sick and I turned away, trying to fight the current and make a stealthy exit. I don't even know why I was there. What good is a cut man when the whole point is to make your fighters bleed? The noise in the room turned into kind of a static for me, like trying to find a radio station out in the boonies. The cheers, the roars, flesh and bone striking flesh and bone, the wet sopping, it melded together into one distortion.

My fingers touched the gold doorknob when something broke through the mess. It was scarcely a whisper, but it cut through the fog of the crowd as if it came through a bullhorn. Pembrose. He was saying something in that weird language I'd heard fragments of in past fights. I turned from the door and somehow, through the crowd, saw Pembrose, smug little grin on his face, revealing a double set of teeth, yellow and red. He noticed my eavesdropping and turned to regard me. His grin widened. His eyes flashed a light that I'd never seen before. It came out in the same gray that floated about in Duane's eyes, but more intense, vibrant in a way that exuded insanity and rage, the very same that held the crowd in its clutches. I tried to look away but couldn't. Pembrose had entranced me and he'd no intentions of simply letting me walk away from it all. The gray light opened a doorway within his eyes, leading me into a place of swirling gases and foam. It went on forever. I could wander for a thousand lifetimes in there and never find the end. I wouldn't be alone there. No, in the bowers, in the dark, there were...*things*. I didn't see them, but I felt their presence, and they mine. Whatever they were, whatever they had in mind for me, I wanted no part in it. I shook my head and cried and tried to break free.

*"Watch then, Mr. Brava. Bear witness and give the world your testimony, be you unready for the beyond."*

The other place, the *beyond*, faded away, taking Pembrose along with it. What he left behind for me...

...it was Hell.

# Chapter 10

I'D BEEN TO WAR. I'd seen death, violent, pointless death. Hell, I made a *living* off blood.

None of that prepared me for what I saw.

It started with Duane. "The Angry One." Whatever was happening, it unleashed what I'd only caught glimpses of before. He grabbed Ivan's arm and, before Ivan could do anything about it, he bent it in a way God did not intend. The bones crackled as they broke apart, then there was this wet ripping as the jagged edges ripped through the skin. The big Slav ceased his attack and regarded his mangled arm as if it were some kind of mistake, like it belonged to someone else and not him. He slid off Duane and said something in his native tongue; I couldn't tell you what it was, but I can tell you it was the last thing he'd ever say. Duane rose to his feet and slugged him in the jaw, knocking him to the ground. From there, he pounced on him, forgoing the use of his fists in favor of his teeth. Blood spurted from underneath his jaw as Ivan screamed.

Something hit me then and I fell to the ground. I looked up in time to see a shoe coming at me, and then it all went hazy. I caught glimpses of what was happening, or *had already happened*. I truly don't know if I was seeing it play out before me or if I was watching a memory.

Everyone in the room, the elites, the paragons, the so-called "Captains of Industry," were at each other's throats. The violence they'd bore witness to had infected them, turned them into the very thing they'd come to see: murderers.

To my left, a media mogul had his thumbs buried in the eyes of his young date for the evening. She carved deep gouges in his face and neck as she fought him for life, failing. There were no screams from either of them, but only high-pitched, manic *giggling*.

To my right, the governor and the chief of the state police, having finished stomping a state senator's head into a mushy, skull-clumped puddle, turned on each other, each man seeking to strangle the other while they, too, laughed.

Scenes like this played out across the suite. A pack of debutantes disemboweled their sugar daddy and then strangled each other with his soppy entrails. The son from one of the premier families in the country (having been floated as a future presidential candidate) cracked open his father's skull and picked pieces of his brain out, eating them like appetizers.

Gunshots rang out. The smell of burnt gunpowder mixing with the blood. For a moment I was back in the frozen mud of Korea, holding my helmet and screaming for God to save me. I ducked my head down, closed my eyes, and waited for the blackness to come, as it had always been coming for me since that Montessi fight.

It didn't, of course. Here I sit telling you this incredible story, right?

Instead of a bullet to my head, I got hands underneath my arms lifting me to my feet. I opened my eyes to see two of Applebaum's goons holding me in place, blood decorating their faces like tattoos. They had the same wide-eyed craziness I'd seen in the other people as they were tearing each other apart, but it was different somehow; diluted, I guess, like whatever was causing it had weakened. They dragged me across the room—my feet bumping against corpse after corpse—to Applebaum himself.

He stood over one of the guests. The poor bastard had stripped to his skivvies and was rubbing entrails and blood into his bare skin with one hand and, with the other, he had someone's foot—a woman's, still in her heel—and gnawed at it like a dog with a big soup-bone.

"Bill," Applebaum said, letting out a big sigh, like he was *relieved* to see me. "You know who he is?"

I couldn't find my words at that point, so I shook my head. "He was set to be the next big motion picture star, Bill. Got a picture coming out next week that they say ought to win him one of those Academy Awards, he's so good in it. Man had the world by the balls. More money than God, broads, cars, you name it. Look at him now, Bill, look at him now."

The actor had managed to bite the big toe off. He worked it around his jaw, eyes darting about when Applebaum blew half his head off. He'd win that Academy Award too—posthumously, one of the very few they've ever given out, so I'm told.

Applebaum nodded to his goons and they let loose of me. He put the gun in his holster and pulled out a crumpled pack of smokes. His hands shook as he lit one. This was the first time I'd seen him in such a state, even with the increasing amount of nose candy he tooted. Murray Applebaum wasn't one to display any kind of vulnerability. In his line of work, that generally meant being found in a dumpster. He walked over to an upturned chair, lifted it upright, and sat down, brushing away the gore as best he could. Not that it mattered. He was bathed in it. His spiffy suit was ruined, his smoked glasses even darker now. He sucked half the cigarette down in one go and exhaled it in a huge plume before running his hands through his hair, the snow-white streaking pink and red.

"Jesus... What the hell happened, Bill?"

"Pembrose," I said.

Applebaum looked at me with raised eyebrows. He shook his head and laughed without joy once. "Pembrose."

"I don't know *what* or *how*, Mr. Applebaum, only that this was him."

Applebaum played with the ring on his pinky, regarding it the way a man lost in the desert regards a glass of water, finally flipping it open to reveal the white powder within. He raised it to his nose, hesitating for a moment before taking a long sniff.

"Marcus, bourbon," he said to one of the goons, who stepped gingerly over the bodies and blood to the bar. I heard clanking as he struggled to find a glass and bottle not ruined by the violence. "You been straight with me, Bill? I thought I told you to tell me everything that happened in that mausoleum, no matter how trivial or strange."

"I-I did that, Mr. Applebaum. I swear on my mother's eyes! He kept me in the dark about a lot, showing me only what I needed to see to report back to you."

The goon Marcus placed two fingers of bourbon in Applebaum's hand. He sipped it, grimacing. "Is that a fact?"

"He kept himself locked away in the goddamn basement most of the time, him and Duane. God knows what they were doing down there."

"The basement."

I nodded. "I couldn't get in. Pembrose put up more locks when he found out I was poking around after..."

"After?" Applebaum cocked an eyebrow. "After what?"

"After that girl went missing," I said. "Dolores."

"You think Pembrose had something to do with that?"

I told Applebaum about the string of missing women in town, how they all disappeared similarly to Dolores. He nodded and drank his bourbon, finishing it as I finished my theory. "I think it was Duane who took the women. Pembrose allowed it; some kind of reward or what have you for doing what he was told. Whatever it was, whatever *this* was, the answers are going to be somewhere in that basement."

"All right, Bill. I guess we're going to the basement."

"Mr. Applebaum, I-I don't need to go down there, do I? I mean, I'm just a cut man. This...magic or whatever, it's way beyond me."

"It's way beyond *anyone*, Bill. You think I want to go chasing that tall creep into his lair like he's fucking Dracula? We're in it, Bill. There's no escaping it, no hiding from it. We're going down there. We were *always* going down there."

And so on we went, out of the slaughterhouse and down to Applebaum's Cadillac on our way to Pembrose's mansion and the basement. A more motley crew of heroes you'd never see by far. A couple of gangsters and a cut man off to confront the monsters.

We'd have been better off pulling onto the highway and driving straight out of town.

# Chapter 11



"Christ, this place stinks! How'd you stand it, Bill?"

Applebaum gagged the second we walked in the front door, unlocked and partly open. His goons, Marcus and Bruce, retched the instant they hit the front stoop, dry-heaving and doubling over. It was worse than any point in my time living there. I stopped, ran back to the car, and opened the glove box. Applebaum kept a bottle or two of his aftershave in there, potent stuff that reeked of chemicals and what was supposed to be "a hint of Florida sunshine," according to the label. In reality, it smelled more like a Florida swamp, but at that point, I'd take it. I tore down the nearest set of drapes in the mansion I could grab and set to work tearing little strips and dousing them with the stuff.

"Should help," I said, passing them out to each man.

"What the hell is that? A sewer line?" the goon, Bruce, asked.

"You ever smell shit like that?" Marcus replied between deep inhales of the cologne.

The mansion was empty, *quiet*. I swore we'd walk in and face Rumnian servants aiming guns at us, or that the digging sounds that plagued my nights for months would be deafening. There was nothing. Other than the rushed footprints in the dust on the floor, you'd never have thought people had even been in there for years.

"The basement, Bill," Applebaum said. "If you would."

I led them toward the quadruple-locked door. Applebaum's demeanor had changed on the ride over from the penthouse. He had a fresh set of clothes brought from one of his properties and, after a quick stop to wash the blood from his face and hair (best he could; it still had a dull pink hue to it), he emerged almost reborn. The ashtray in the back seat of the car was overflowing with cashed butts by the time we pulled up, and he did take two or three long toots from his party ring before getting out, but I can't sit here and say I blame him the one bit. I was so scared, I was shaking. At least they all had guns; wouldn't give me one when I asked. Bruce shook his head as he loaded a magazine into his machine gun. Marcus replied by racking his shotgun. I didn't even bother asking Applebaum.

"Here," I said, coming around the corner by the main staircase to the basement door. "It's here."

"Bruce. Bust it open."

Bruce handed his machine gun to Marcus and pulled a crowbar from his jacket. The frame splintered and the locks gave way, showering Bruce with wood and plaster; he wiped it off his suit with a grimace. A fresh wave of the stench hit us as the door wobbled open. Not even Applebaum's cologne offered much protection. We stood there, bent over and retching for five minutes before it lessened enough for us to head down.

The stairs were metal grates bolted into the foundation, announcing our arrival with hollow echoes. The basement floor was earth; soft, black soil that felt like walking on the beach. The goons, in their shiny shoes, slipped more than once. Thankfully, Pembrose left the lights burning (none of us had thought to bring a single flashlight) in the form of small torches that hung in sconces made of iron along the walls.

The basement was huge. A few broken chairs and empty boxes were scattered here and there, but the place was mainly empty, except for a trail of footprints.

"Guess we know where everyone went," Applebaum said.

We followed the trail, finding nothing, seeing nothing but the dimly lit blackness of the basement. We must have wandered around there, kicking up black dirt all over ourselves, for close to ten minutes before we came across the "training room."

"Jesus Christ," Marcus said. "What the hell is that?"

What "that" was was a boxing ring. The skeleton remained—turnbuckles, ropes, and canvas—but square in the center, instead of blue canvas, was a hole. No. More like something from outer space fell down and crashed into it. The edges were charred and jagged as if they'd been burnt, not excavated.

We climbed into the ring and stood around the hole.

"Guess we found the source of the smell," Bruce said, gagging.

The hole smelled worse than any other place in the house. I could see clouds of whatever it was shimmering in the faint torchlight.

"Where the hell does it lead?"

"Down, dummy."

"Har-har, Bruce," Marcus said. "Why would they dig here? What's down there?"

"Who gives a shit," Applebaum said. "These freaks went down there, so we're going too. Nobody crosses Murray Applebaum."

Both the goons nodded and zipped their lips. Applebaum knelt by the hole despite the death stench. He took off his smoked lenses and squinted into the gloom for a bit, pausing only to take a bit of powdered courage from his party ring. "There's some kind of tunnel," he said, rubbing some coke on his gums. "I can see light."

"How'd they even get down there?" Bruce said.

"With that." Applebaum pointed at a rope ladder anchored into the canvas in between Bruce's feet.

"Oh. Right."

"So, we go?" Marcus said.

"We go. Bill, you're first."

I glanced at Applebaum and, upon seeing him wave me on with his gun, I decided against lodging a complaint. He'd no clue as to what lay in that hole and wasn't man enough to confront it head-on, so I was to be the sacrificial goat. I cursed his family back a couple generations as I worked my way down the ladder. Damn thing was soaked to the touch, more sticky than slippery, like that feeling when you get old chewing gum on your hands from a seat on the subway. The thing was about as sturdy as a shrub in a hurricane, too. I swung all around the hole, colliding off one wall and then bouncing into the next for every rung I went down. Clumps of earth assailed me, getting into my ears, nose, my eyes and mouth. I was blinking tears and coughing like I belonged in the TB ward by the time I got halfway down; at least, I *thought* it was halfway down. The fact of the matter was, I had no idea how far down the damn thing went, if I was going to climb for five minutes or if the ladder was going to run out and I'd be left dangling off the last rung as my legs flailed about in the abyss.

The latter didn't happen, fortunately. My feet hit solid ground after I'd climbed fifty rungs worth of the ladder. I gave it a tug to let the gangsters know I made it down, then gave a look around to figure where in the hell I actually *was*.

The bottom of the hole was more loose soil, swallowing my feet to the ankle, and ending at some kind of *doorway* unearthed by Pembrose's excavations. It was enormous, stretching up at least three stories and near that in width. Along the interior were pictures carved into the metal. To me, they looked like frantic, angry scratches, as if whatever was locked inside was trying to break free through brute force. I'd only taken a few steps inside the structure when Marcus landed behind me, cursing a blue streak.

"What in the name of Jesus Fucking Christ is that?" he said, beating dirt from his suit.

"You're asking *me?*" I said.

"You lived with these freaks," he said.

I turned away as Bruce and Applebaum made their way down. The tunnel was lit by some strange lights hidden behind gates cut out of the stone walls. They burned like torch-fire but gave off no heat or smoke. The scratches stopped around thirty paces inside, and the walls turned to a flawless, reflective surface. It felt warm to the touch and yet earthy like stone.

"See anything up there, Bill?" Applebaum said as he walked inside the door. He regarded the door with a moment of awe that quickly turned into primal fear. He and I locked gazes and I saw it. He was thinking that he'd hate to meet the thing that this place was built to hold, same as me. His eyes flashed danger to me and he flexed his grip on the gun to emphasize the point that it would be very bad for me should I make mention of his momentary lapse.

"It's a tunnel," I said, turning from him as he tooted more cocaine. "It goes on for a ways. No clue how far, but looks long."

"Well, there's only one way they could've gone, so that's where we're going, even if we have to walk all goddamn night."

"If you say so, Murray," I said.

"*Mr. Applebaum,* Bill. Even down here."

We walked in silence. The tunnel shared none of its secrets. Nothing but smooth walls lit by the strange lights as far as we could see. The only indicator that we were actually moving forward was that the rope ladder grew smaller and smaller until it was a tiny dot behind us.

We walked until our legs were rubber and we were breathing heavy. Bruce and Marcus removed their suit coats and had pitted out their undershirts. I, too, was a mess of sweat, aching feet, and weariness. Only Applebaum seemed lively. His coiffed hair, still perfect, and nary a drop of sweat upon his brow. He kept pushing me forward, bringing the gun up if I turned to protest.

"This is ridiculous," I said. "We've been walking forever and aren't any closer to finding them."

"You want to give up, Bill? Go home and pretend it was all a bad dream?"

"Yeah, *Murray,* I might want to do that! We have no clue what we're dealing with here."

"Nobody, and I mean *nobody,* gets over on Murray Applebaum. If that means we gotta walk under the goddamn Atlantic to find this prick, then walk we shall. I'll go even farther to see the life run out of his eyes, so don't *test* me, Bill. You're in this until I say otherwise, and I am not saying otherwise, understand?"

"At least it don't stink anymore," Marcus said with a shrug. "I mean, it kinda smells like Revere Beach at low tide."

"Shut up, both of you."

"Wait. He's right," I said. "I *do* smell the ocean."

# Chapter 12

Where we came out wasn't Revere Beach.

"Boss," Marcus said, letting his shotgun fall limp against his thigh. "Why is the ocean in the sky?"

Applebaum didn't answer. Couldn't. He stood next to me staring at the same impossibility, trying to wrack his brain to make the thing he was seeing make any semblance of sense, and, like the rest of us, he was failing.

The water, blue-green, near the color of emeralds, the churning waves breaking against shore, hung over our heads where the sky and clouds ought to have been. The waves broke against the side of the structure we were in. We felt the spray on our faces. It was oily to the touch and tasted foul, brackish like a swamp. We heard the call of gulls and even saw a few if we squinted, seeing them as tiny dots of white, floating below the water, darting up and then down again, their beaks presumably filled with food. What that was, I didn't care to find out.

I don't know how long we stood there, but it was long enough for Marcus' mind to break apart like the waves above us. I heard a giggle and turned to find he had his face in his hands, laughing and laughing. I'd be lying if I said I didn't eyeball his shotgun lying on the rocky ground. With that, I'd have been able to get back in the tunnel and be well gone before they could do anything about it.

I didn't get the chance.

It happened so fast: Marcus' death. I've seen how fast a man can die in the war, sure, but I never got used to it the way some others did. To be here, breathing, thinking one second, and then, *poof*?

Sorry, I'm woolgathering here.

Marcus stripped to the waist. He was crying, crying *and* laughing. He took off his shoes and socks and ran to the edge. I don't know why, but that was the part that scared me the most. Applebaum shouted at him, but there was no reaching the poor bastard; not then. He screamed, "*I WANT TO SWIM IN THE SKY!*" and then he jumped.

Bruce was the closest to the edge. He whispered the Lord's Prayer and turned away. Applebaum edged past him and looked for himself. "Christ on the cross..." he said.

Marcus didn't swim in the sky. He plunged into darkness. Whatever was at the bottom was covered in a shroud of black fog. A Marcus-shaped hole opened in it as he passed through, only to be enveloped moments later by the churning mists. His screams carried up.

We heard them for hours.

Oh, my plan to liberate myself with the shotgun? That went to pot before I could make a move for it. Applebaum snatched it up after taking a long snort of his cocaine; the last of it he had.

"I'll take that, Bill," he said and checked the shells. He held it across his chest, staring at me.

Before us were a dozen smaller tunnels leading to parts unknown. I could only imagine the Hells that lay at the end of each one, but I knew that we were going to head down one of them, no matter what.

But which led to Pembrose and Duane?

I walked before one tunnel that was covered in fungus and mushrooms the color of bloody skin. The caps seemed to *follow* me as I walked past, watching, eager for me to come and see; I kept moving.

The inside of another tunnel was overtaken by a root system. Teeth of all sorts stuck out of the roots—themselves made from stone—budding like flowers.

"Which one, Bill?" Applebaum said. He had to shout to be heard over the still-falling Marcus.

I was damned if I knew. In that moment, I didn't know. I was going to do the ol' *eenie-meanie* trick and stall for time when I smelled it.

Duane's blood.

That baked sewage and rotting fish stench had been living in my nostrils for months on end. It permeated out of one of the tunnels so thick I swear I could almost *see* the plumes. The tunnel was one of the less terrifying, but only slightly so. There was no light beyond that of the chamber leaking in, and that only made it a foot or two before the dark swallowed it whole. On the edge of the dark, there was blood spatter. Duane's.

"It's this one," I said. "But there's no light."

"Then I suppose you'll have to watch your step, Bill."

Applebaum, the son of a bitch he was, gave me a tiny nudge with the barrel of the shotgun. Bruce watched me go in, shrugging his broad shoulders as I walked past him in some kind of attempt to intimidate me or what have you. It's almost funny as I think about it now. What could be *more* frightening than walking blind into absolute darkness?

I was about to find out. We all were.

# Chapter 13

THERE WEREN'T ANY MONSTERS or things that go bump in the night in the tunnel. Other than the slowness of our trek down it (I kept both hands against the walls and felt ahead by sweeping my feet in front of me), the trip was uneventful. Bruce hummed some showtune to himself; I forget the name. Applebaum didn't make a sound.

After a while, a pinpoint of white light appeared in the distance. It felt like that would be the time when the evil that Pembrose and Duane were a part of decided to act against us. My heart pounded against my chest so hard it made my back teeth hurt. A cold sweat soaked me to the bone. The light was blinding the closer we got to it, so much so that we couldn't see what was beyond. I hesitated at the darkness' edge. The fear undid me, finally. After the war, the threat of death from Applebaum, living in that goddamn house with Pembrose, it was taking one last step to the big reveal that my brain refused to allow my body to perform.

Applebaum had Bruce give me an *assist.* The big man did so by kicking me square in the ass, sending me sprawling onto my face.

My vision cleared, revealing some kind of laboratory, one crossed with a morgue. Empty platforms carved out of smooth stone lined the floor, surrounded by heavy leather curtains, more at home hanging from a butcher's chest than here. Blood was... It was *everywhere.* Droplets swelled at the tips of the stalactites overhead, dripping down like sprinkles of rain. I picked my hands up after finding them sunk wrist-deep in a pool of it. I staggered to my feet, only to trip over something, landing on my ass in the blood-swamp. It was a body; one of the Rumnian servants. They were *flayed*, damn near down to the bone. I couldn't tell if they were male or female; only way I knew they were from Rumney was the smell that came off them, the distinctness of it. I stared into their dead eyes and began to scream, only to find a hand clamped over my mouth.

"Don't make another sound," Applebaum said. I didn't hear him approach.

Following the end of his finger, I saw what was making him so cautious. There was an outline, a protrusion from the other side of the curtains, pushing out from the very top and then disappearing. A heavy exhale followed, as did heavier footsteps walking away from us farther into the lab, sounding like metal scraping against bone. The curtains didn't quite reach the ground, so I caught a glimpse of the thing as it walked away. It had no feet to speak of, but *hooves*...hooves made from *teeth*.

I don't know how long we crouched there—Applebaum's well-manicured hand over my mouth while Bruce crouched, aiming his gun, trying not to shake. The hand remained in place until the creature's footsteps turned mute.

"What the *fuck*, boss?" Bruce said.

"Bill?"

"How am *I* supposed to know what that was?" I said.

"Christ. It must be twenty feet tall!"

"Don't shit yourself, boys," Applebaum said. "It doesn't matter how tall it is, it'll bleed all the same if it gets between me and Pembrose."

Applebaum made us go deeper into the lab. It was difficult to keep quiet with the blood being ankle-deep in most places, so the going was slow. The curtained area stretched on for a long ways. The closed spaces, the way the leather seemed to absorb all the light and air, leaving behind that of guts, brought me back to the MASH units from the war. I had many friends go in one of those green tents only to come out in bags. I was lucky in that regard, but walking through that place, blood soaking through my shoes into my skin, I began to wonder if I really *was*.

# Chapter 14

We came upon a survivor on one of the altars.

It was Dolores. What was left of her.

They'd pulled the veins out and attached them to this odd, egg-shaped apparatus on the ground. They'd opened her arms up below her biceps, peeled the skin and muscle back, then pulled the veins free from her body, leaving them intact and, more or less, functional, save for where they made their cuts, severing them from pumping anything to her hands. Her legs had been sliced open along her thighs, splitting them down the middle. The ends were then attached to tubes protruding out from the egg. These reminded me of melted sugar, charred black and sticky-like. Dolores' blood flowed from her through these thick tubes into the egg, which gave off pulses as it absorbed it.

"Is she still alive?" Bruce said.

Dolores the debutante was still amongst the living, although it seemed like more of a curse than a blessing to me. Her eyes were wide open and unblinking. Her mouth twitched at the corners and, every so often, her lips seemed to try to form words only to fail halfway through. There was swelling around her eyes and her nose had been broken. Seemed to me that she put up a struggle when she saw what Pembrose and Duane intended, or maybe they beat her up for the sake of cruelty; I can't say.

"Look," Applebaum said. "There's more of them."

We counted seven; two of them had been dead for some time. These included the two men with Dolores the night she disappeared, and the remaining missing women from the papers. All were cut up the same as Dolores and attached to eggs of their own. All were unresponsive.

"I'm tired of you playing dumb, Bill," Applebaum said. "You're going to tell me what that is or I'm going to strap you down and feed you to one of these eggs myself."

My eyes wandered from the shotgun aimed at my guts to the egg near Dolores. It wasn't made of anything I could recognize. It felt hard and soft to the touch at the same time. My fingers sank into it, only to have the indents smooth themselves out after I removed them. There were symbols etched or carved into the bottom. I looked at these and knew I'd seen them before. In that odd book, *On Lemuria: Thoughts, Theories, and the Truth on the Lost Continent.*

It was in a strange section of the book that didn't really seem to belong, but the author, Norris, felt it worthy of inclusion. It went on for three pages, pages filled by these symbols, some drawn in crude, bold scratches, others stamped in place. They were part of the Lemurian alphabet, one of several they had, each one serving a distinct purpose. This particular one being that of a "hidden source of power," only to be wielded by the most learned of scholars.

I told this to Applebaum, explaining it as best as I could. He looked as if I'd got done telling him—in graphic detail—how I deflowered his sister.

"That's it? This is some kind of, what...*magic?*"

"Not sure how that's not in the realm of possibility for you, *Murray,*" I said. "Have you *not* been seeing any of this?"

Applebaum waved me off. As he did, something shimmered in front of him. I waved my own hand in the air and saw it again. My hand came back damp and, upon looking at my palm, I saw the faintest traces of red. *Blood.* The blood from Dolores and the others. It hung in the air all around us, all but totally invisible. The concentration was heaviest near the eggs, but faded the farther away you got. I scraped some dirt from the floor and tossed it in the air. The blood appeared as clumpy lumps of mud, revealing a distinct direction, leading from this section, underneath the thick leather apron.

"If they're still anywhere in this Hell, I'd say it's going to be at the end of that," I said.

Applebaum took the lead, pushing past Bruce and me. It was hard to keep up with the trail of blood in the air; we had to stop twice to throw more dirt into the air to make sure we'd not lost it.

Underneath the apron, the cavern narrowed to a tunnel that we could only walk through one by one. It felt like the walls were actively fighting us, like they were moving closer and closer together to squash us into paste.

"*YOU!*"

There he was. Pembrose. Flanked by the surviving Rumnian servants, next to a large red cauldron. The blood trail hung overhead, moving like the sky-borne sea that Marcus died trying to reach, toward the cauldron, emptying into it like a gentle rain trickling through a gutter. Behind it stood Duane. He held a large wooden staff and was stirring the contents of the cauldron, staring into it with a blank expression.

"Mr. Applebaum," Pembrose said. "Ah, and Mr. Brava, and...I don't believe I've had the pleasure of meeting your large friend holding the machine gun."

Applebaum started shooting; Bruce followed a split-second afterward. No talking, no threats, not like in the gangster movies. I didn't even have time to duck for cover. I froze in place, hands over my ears, and watched the whole thing go down, which went completely against my old Army training. I did that in Korea, I would have been bleeding out into the grass the second I stepped off the plane. The machine gun sprayed while the shotgun roared. Burnt powder mixed with the blood, filling my mouth with the taste of metal and souring my stomach enough to the point I fell to my knees, dry-heaving.

I saw bullets and slugs tear through the Rumnian servants, geysers of that strange-colored blood of theirs exploded in their torsos, arms, legs. One poor bastard, the man I think was in charge of making breakfast for me, got it in the eye. His head snapped back and the blood that sprayed up from the wound landed back on his face like a gentle spring rain.

Pembrose? He stood still, smiling and shaking his head, bemused at what Applebaum was doing. The rounds hit him, but there were no visible wounds. The only indicator being that lithe frame of his twisting this way or that.

They paused to reload, and all the servants were lying on the ground, dead or on their way to it. Only Pembrose and Duane were untouched.

"You men," Pembrose said. "You men and your *guns*. It's a falsity, you know. The power you believe you possess whilst holding one of those crude projectiles? A mirage, Mr. Applebaum."

"Bruce? Shoot that prick in the mouth for me, will ya?" Applebaum said, struggling to load slugs into the belly of the shotgun.

Bruce slapped a fresh magazine into his machine gun and strode up to Pembrose, letting off a quick burst as he closed the distance to the same results. Pembrose kept his hands at his sides, smiling wider.

Kid should have run for it. We all should have.

It's weird to talk about the last moments of someone's life, especially when you were present for them. Be it dying from cancer in bed or freezing to death on some goddamn hill thousands of miles from home, you take a bit of that person with you and those last moments become a part of you, as much as your fingers or nose. I imagine if you told Bruce he only had three more steps to take in his life, he'd have cursed you for a liar.

That was it. Three steps.

Duane intercepted him as he raised the gun to Pembrose's face. He grabbed it by the barrel and yanked it out of Bruce's grip, tossing it deep into the chamber. Bruce was surprised, but he got over it fast enough to pull out a switchblade he had in his pocket. Duane was faster. I never really saw that speed in his fights. He always played the role of the bruiser, the heavy-handed slugger. Watching him take control of Bruce and subsequently take him apart? Kid was holding back.

Duane broke both of Bruce's arms like they were made out of candy, bending them until the elbows snapped and bone stuck out through the fabric of his jacket. He then lifted him over his head and onto his shoulders like he weighed nothing at all. Duane carried him across the way a bit, catching glances with me as he walked on by. The gray flecks were bright as the sun; I heard that clicking of his tongue too. "The Angry One" was in the driver's seat and Christ if that didn't have me prepping to meet Saint Peter.

He stopped before this hollow rock formation. Inside lay a pool of still black liquid. He shrugged Bruce off his shoulders and he disappeared underneath the stuff. He broke the surface only once, gasping for air and coated in what looked like oil. He didn't have time to scream, for help, for God, before whatever lived in that muck got him. They were fast, rising from all angles around him. Tentacles, dripping with the syrupy goop, wrapped around his body tight and squeezed. I saw one of his eyes pop out of his head before one of the fleshy stalks wrapped around his face and pulled him into the muck.

"Son of a bitch!" Applebaum screamed, firing the shotgun at Pembrose. Pembrose was outright laughing as the slugs bounced off him, landing as smoldering hunks of useless metal at his feet. Applebaum, lost to his rage, kept shooting. *"I'll kill you, you bastard! No one screws with Murray Applebaum!"*

I watched Duane then, worried he'd toss Applebaum, then me, to the tentacles. As a result, I missed seeing the Rumnians' resurrection. They rose to their feet, still bleeding from their gunshot wounds, and swarmed Applebaum, ripping the shotgun from his hands and pulling him to the ground. I saw those smoked lenses disappear underneath a frenzy of grubby fingers, and then he went silent. A few of the group dragged him away—I didn't know if he was dead or not then—and the rest turned to me.

I ran for it, ducking back under the leather aprons and running through the surgical theater, slipping on the bloody mud. The victims lying there, having their blood sucked out, the cave, all of it was streaks of images in my view. I heard the Rumnians behind me, their footsteps like stampeding horses. I made it to the entrance, to the surgical area, could almost touch the opening flaps of the leather dividers, when I felt cold hands around me. I was pulled to the ground and the lights went out.

# Chapter 15

I woke up tied to a rock. I couldn't move a quarter-inch in any direction, could scarcely catch my breath for that matter. Applebaum sat on the ground next to me in the same situation. Blood ran out of his nose and right ear, matting in his hair, which had lost the Brylcreem hold and jutted out in wild angles. The Rumnians stood around us, hands at their sides and with blank stares.

"Welcome back to the realm of the conscious, Mr. Brava."

"Let me go, Pembrose," I said. "I got nothing to do with this—whatever it is. I won't speak a word of it, on my mother's eyes."

"And rob from you the chance to bear witness to something greater than yourself? A bona-fide miracle, one not seen since the days of the Bible?" Pembrose wagged his finger at me. "I think not, Mr. Brava. You were meant to end up here. Who would I be to challenge the will of the universe? Me, a simple boxing manager?"

"Is that all you are, Pembrose?" I said. "I know lots of managers, and none of them can turn an entire room into bloodthirsty monsters."

"True enough, Mr. Brava, and a *fair* point, I must concede. You're cleverer than the others," Pembrose nodded at Applebaum, who moaned in his sleep. "Perhaps that is why I allowed you into my home, to get a peek at how the sausage gets made, so to speak. You spent much time in our library, yes? How did you find Norris' ruminations? Were they illuminating, Mr. Brava?"

"This is insane!" I said. "Lost continents, oceans in the sky, dead people coming back to life... You've done something to me! Drugs or...or *hypnosis*!"

"We both know you don't believe a word of what you just spoke, Mr. Brava. Please don't embarrass yourself any further."

The pitiful thing of it was...he was right. I knew I'd not been given a hot dose or had the whammy put on me. It was all real. It was all happening. And there wasn't a damn thing I could do about it.

Pembrose walked to the cauldron. Duane helped him undress, carefully folding his suit and placing it on the ground. Once he was nude, he walked up a stepstool and stood over the cauldron. The fumes left a rust-colored tinge on his pale skin. He took several deep breaths and then stepped inside. His screams began the instant his toes touched the blood, growing in pitch as he slowly submerged himself. Before he disappeared, I caught a glimpse of the damage the liquid was inflicting upon him. The skin on his neck was all but turned into goop, droplets of it fell into the pot like he was a melting candle. It ate half of his earlobe on one side and the other was actively burning. All the while, Pembrose screamed. This finally, mercifully, stopped once he dunked his head under the surface.

I don't know how long he was under for. Far too long for a normal person to hold their breath. During this, Applebaum woke up and was none too happy to discover he was someone's prisoner. He thrashed against the rock, hollering and cursing the Rumnians and their mothers. This stopped when Duane walked over and popped him in the nose with a stiff jab that snapped Applebaum's head back against the rock, knocking him into a semi-conscious, drooling state.

"Duane, let me go, huh? I got nothing to do with any of this. You know that, you know *me*. Please, Duane, let me go home," I said.

Duane looked me right in the eye, something he never did to anyone save for the opponent in the other corner. The flecks of gray were dimmer now, but they smoldered with a bit of whatever fueled his rage. He had his hands still clenched into fists; a bit of Applebaum's blood dripped onto the floor of the cave.

"You *are* going home," Duane said. "We *all* are."

Before I could say anything else, Pembrose surfaced in the cauldron.

The blood concoction changed him. It'd melted away most of his flesh, but also merged with it, forming a sinewy carapace around his limbs and torso that was an angry orange-red and sizzled as it touched the air, creating sparks around him. He had no face anymore. Instead, he had a protrusion, a blob of drying blood and flesh that happened to form around his skull. A hole tore through the new flesh where the mouth ought to have been, a fleshy nub probed the edges, wagging and flapping in the air obscenely. On the tip lay a lidless eye, gray and bulging. It passed over me, then Applebaum, and then darted around, looking at the Rumnians. Words spoke inside my head from a language I didn't understand. It sounded like gibberish, utter nonsense that grew from a muted whisper to a raging shout until my head felt ready to crack apart.

*Wgah'nagl, llll gn'th'bthnk ng will, way wgah'nagl ahor mgahnnn ehye ahog. Lemuria! throdog Lemuria!!*

One by one, the Rumnians slipped out of their clothes. Once nude, they grabbed handfuls of their skin—around their arms, stomachs, wherever they could grab—and they started...*pulling*. No expressions changed, none made any sounds or signs of pain. Slowly, their skin came off in great, long peels. It was like when you peel an orange, that first wet crunch and then how the tearing reverberates through the whole fruit. The air even misted, but it wasn't citrus that came out, but that terrible murky blood. What lay underneath their skin wasn't anything human. Remember how I told you about what I saw in some of Duane's cuts? That jagged, black stuff that looked like teeth? Well, I was wrong about that. It wasn't teeth. It was part of a pattern, like a frog's.

This was their true form. Dark green skin mottled with patterns of blacks and browns and that slimy, orangey blood. Their black eyes darted about their skulls, looking in all directions, but always coming back to Pembrose. Faint specks of gray and yellow glowed within, burning like leaves in a brushfire. The strange words that raced through my head now came from their mouths, down-turned gray lines of flesh that appeared gouged into their faces that, when open, revealed not one, but two hideous tongues, rolling about like a den of snakes.

*Wgah'nagl, llll gn'th'bthnk ng will, way wgah'nagl ahor mgahnnn ehye ahog. Lemuria! throdog Lemuria!! Wgah'nagl, llll gn'th'bthnk ng will, way wgah'nagl ahor mgahnnn ehye ahog. Lemuria! throdog Lemuria!!*

Duane disappeared while his fellow Rumnians ripped their disguises off, reappearing as the chant began, still wearing his human face and carrying Dolores over his shoulder. Pembrose nodded to him, and his tongue-eye danced in his mouth. Duane placed Dolores down next to me, resting her head on my shoulder. Her eyes and mouth were open, but she wasn't seeing anything. Whatever they'd done to her, it'd hollowed her out.

Duane walked to the spot Pembrose directed him to. He reached out and seemed to try and grab hold of the empty space over his head. He grunted and started to pull and strain. My head hurt something awful during this. My fillings worked themselves free and rattled around my mouth. Blood came out of my nose, my ears. I cried tears of it! The world got fuzzy, blurred, like someone had taken hold of it and was shaking it faster and faster. The chanting reached a fervor. Pembrose leapt out of the cauldron, his body drippings trailing behind him as he walked behind Duane, flapping his melted appendages in excitement.

It came in two cracks, the tearing of the world. The first as Duane's fingers forced their way through, revealing orange-yellow flashes that blinded me as the tear was born. It also broke the rock behind me, inadvertently freeing me. I had enough time to scramble to my hands and knees when the second crack came, knocking me, Dolores, and even Applebaum all the way across the room. It was difficult to tell up from down. I couldn't get my brain to make my legs work the way they were supposed to. This worsened as Duane ripped through the fabric of reality like he was peeling off a scab.

The wound, for what else could I consider it, he left behind pulsated with blinding light. I couldn't make out what lay beyond, nor did I care to. My head felt like it was crumbling and only hastened the more I looked at it. Pembrose and the Rumnians had forgotten all about us. They dropped to their knees, prostrating themselves before the wound, screaming the same gibberish over and over.

*Lemuria! throdog Lemuria!! Lemuria! throdog Lemuria!!*

Pembrose was the first to enter the wound. He caught fire as he approached and was engulfed by the time he walked through. Despite having no tongue anymore, I swear I heard him screaming as he disappeared into the flashing light. After him, the Rumnians walked through, single file, chanting softly. None of them caught fire or seemed to be disturbed by the energy coming from the wound.

Despite my head feeling like an ice cream left on the stoop, I got my bearings and made to run, only to trip over Dolores' prone body. Her open, unseeing eyes stared at the wound in the world, the light dancing about in the emptiness of them. I couldn't leave her there to whatever fate Duane had in mind. I picked her up and ran for the way out; she was lighter than air.

"D-Don't leave me, Bill… *Please…*"

Applebaum was trapped underneath a pile of rubble. He reached for me with a quivering hand. I could even see some tears in his eyes. Murray Fucking Applebaum, brought low after all. It wasn't as satisfying as I thought it would have been. I placed Dolores on the ground and helped Applebaum crawl out of the rubble, trying to make as little noise as I could, for Duane lingered near the wound, watching his fellow Rumnians march through. If he saw us trying to lam it with his prize, his *bride,* well, we'd be wishing to be thrown into the pool of tentacles.

I helped Applebaum to his feet when he turned to look at the wound, seeing it for the first time. He screamed until he started laughing and kept doing that until his voice gave out and could only let out a dry clucking.

"The Angry One" heard.

Brushing Applebaum aside like he wasn't even there, Duane was upon me before I could say a word. I lay on the ground looking into those inhuman eyes, the gray flecks burning hot. His hands squeezed my throat and things got quiet; a ghost of my gurgles haunted my ears, but that was it. His skin had cracks in it. A big tear ran down his face, splitting it down the middle to reveal the slimy frog skin underneath. Christ, if that awful bloody black stuff didn't start falling on me. It went in my open mouth (not that it went any farther, thanks to Duane), in my eyes, up my nose.

The strangest thing happened next. Instead of *my* life flashing before my eyes on the way to stand before St. Peter, I saw *Duane's.* Not the whole thing, but glimpses, kinda like the previews for coming attractions they show at the movies. I saw Duane meeting Pembrose for the first time and I saw the deal being made. In the next one, Duane was strapped down while Pembrose worked on him with varying tools and knives, hacking away bits of him and collecting the results. Then, it was Pembrose in a rage, standing over smashed lab equipment before one of the altars, actively weeping in despair. The next vision showed Pembrose and Duane in the mansion—Duane overseeing the equipment and furniture being moved in by other Rumnians while Pembrose sat in the library, stacks upon stacks of books scattered all around him. Then Pembrose dancing in joy, holding Duane by the shoulders, telling him he had the answer. Then, Duane training for a fight, then being punched in the face, and then, back in the chair with Pembrose collecting his blood.

*"It must be your rage, Mr. Jones. Collecting samples from you willingly does not activate the wondrous properties in your blood that we require. You must be in violent conflict for it to be active. Why, look at your eyes! They're beautiful when they glow with such anger!"*

I went through each and every fight Duane had, felt every punch received *and* landed, felt the invasiveness of Pembrose's tool scraping around inside the wounds, wounds that I healed!

Next, it went to a car wreck. The three occupants were banged up, but unharmed. I recognized the playboys, recognized Dolores, and witnessed what may have been her last conscious vision. She screamed and scratched, but Duane was too powerful. He took them to Pembrose, helped strap their veins to that egg contraption, then dutifully sat for more blood collection.

*"We've nearly enough now, Mr. Jones. I take it you've chosen your reward in the girl. A fitting prize for bringing us all home indeed. The mystics of Lemuria shall be able to restore your dear, departed wife to you in this vessel, but the current inhabitant? I'm afraid she will bear the cost with the obliteration of her soul."*

Duane dropped me. I slipped in and out of consciousness all while Applebaum kept laughing. Visions of his past kept coming, but were blurry without the direct connection. I saw him take the other women, what *he* did when Pembrose retired for the evening. Finally, I saw a woman, a Rumnian I'd never seen before. She lay in a bed, Duane holding her hand, tears staining his face as she breathed her last. His wife.

Duane lifted Dolores and walked to the wound. I clawed at the ground, trying to stop him. I wasn't fast enough. I could only watch as Duane "The Angry One" Jones left this world for another, taking what remained of Dolores with him.

The wound closed up behind him, blinking out of existence with one last blip of light.

# Chapter 16

We got out of there eventually, Applebaum and me. Not that he was much help in that department. He could walk, could take basic instructions, but he was gone, except for the laughing. He *wouldn't* stop, no matter what I said or did. Even smacked him around a bit, but that brought only a moment's peace before he started sniggering and giggling again. I could've left him behind, sure, but thinking of all the nightmares we experienced and the countless others lurking in other unexplored parts, I realized I couldn't live with myself. Applebaum was a criminal, but not even he deserved that fate.

He's still kicking, Murray; just turned ninety-seven. He's been a ward of the state since we got back and has to be doped up pretty much around the clock, otherwise the laughing starts and he's unable to stop. Still got that beautiful head of hair, too.

As for me, I got out of the fight game after all that. Did odd jobs for a bit, sweeping floors, bartending, construction, until I managed to get on at the library as an assistant, and I've been there ever since. I got a little office in the back where no one ever bothers me. Most nights I stay there, reading until the sun comes up. Pretty much anything I can get my hands on—lots of romances, as they tend to have happy (or happier) endings.

I don't sleep much. Duane and Pembrose wait for me there, along with the others that went through that wound in the world. Dolores is there too, but I know that it's not her, not anymore. Her eyes match Duane's and the flecks of gray glow so bright I can't look at them for long. They stare at me from that place, Lemuria, beckoning me to come forth.

The mansion's still there, abandoned and forsaken by even the most desperate of street people. It's within walking distance of the library. I could get there in a half-hour; twenty minutes if I hustle. I can see the basement, the tunnels, the sea in the sky, all of it as if I were only there minutes ago. I think the wound would re-open for me, should I stand before it.

Maybe I'll go and see. One of these days.

# About the Author

KYLE RADER doesn't color inside the lines and thinks the greatest sin a writer can commit is to bore his or her readers. He is the author of several novels, including *My BFF Satan* and *Four Bullets*. He lives in New Hampshire with his wife, son, and dog, and the last time he boxed someone he got knocked out.

CUT MAN TO THE STARS, BILL BRAVA, FINDS HIMSELF CAUGHT BETWEEN A CORRUPT BOXING PROMOTER AND A FIGHTER OF FRIGHTENING POWER THAT CANNOT BE DEFEATED, UNLESS HE CHOOSES TO BE. DESCENDING INTO THE BARE KNUCKLE FIGHTING ARENA WITH THE BOXER KNOWN AS THE ANGRY ONE, HE COMES FACE TO FACE WITH A TERRIFYING EVIL.

CAN BILL DODGE THE BULLET OF A KILLER AND ESCAPE THE MADDENING, SINISTER GRIP OF AN UNFATHOMABLE TERROR?

A COSMIC HORROR NOVELLA FROM ONE OF THE NEWEST VOICES IN HORROR.

BURIAL BOOKS LLC
WWW.BURIALBOOKS.COM

# MAPLE LANE

## MATTHEW MCCONKEY